EGG
ISLAND

EGG
ISLAND

SARA FLEMINGTON

Publisher: Scott Fraser | Acquiring editor: Russell Smith
Cover designer: Laura Boyle
Cover image: field and sky: Dembee Tsogoo; gas pump: Nikola Johnny Mirkovic; clouds: Michael & Diane Weidne

Library and Archives Canada Cataloguing in Publication

Title: Egg Island / Sara Flemington.
Names: Flemington, Sara, author.
Identifiers: Canadiana (print) 20210291788 | Canadiana (ebook) 2021029180X | ISBN 9781459749351 (softcover) | ISBN 9781459749368 (PDF) | ISBN 9781459749375 (EPUB)
Classification: LCC PS8611.L435 E44 2022 | DDC C813/.6—dc23

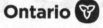

We acknowledge the support of the Canada Council for the Arts and the Ontario Arts Council for our publishing program. We also acknowledge the financial support of the Government of Ontario, through the Ontario Book Publishing Tax Credit and Ontario Creates, and the Government of Canada.

Printed and bound in Canada.

Rare Machines, an imprint of Dundurn Press
1382 Queen Street East
Toronto, Ontario, Canada M4L 1C9
dundurn.com, @dundurnpress ✗ f ◎

For my parents

I
..

BY THE TIME I arrived at the first gas station my shoulders were rubbed raw from the straps of my backpack. My T-shirt and bra all soaked through with sweat. The old man behind the counter asked where I was headed and why the heck I was walking to get there on a day hotter than heck.

I answered, "Because I have feet. Can I use your washroom?"

He pointed past me, where a tall kid about my age with messy brown hair and a studded belt stocked dripping cans of Sprite into a fridge.

The old man said, "Colt, show her the washroom."

Colt looked over his shoulder. He looked me in the eyes like he was going to love me then murder me, then spend the rest of his life building a shrine for me.

"This way," he said.

He led me out back and around the corner to a busted white door with a hole at the bottom. Kicked it open, just above that hole. I stepped past him and let the door shut behind me. There was no lock. I held my breath, rinsed my face and armpits in the sink, ran some water through my hair, then pulled my shorts to my knees and squatted over the toilet. Colt kicked at the gravel outside the door. I hovered, waiting. Then he started humming. I started to pee, and he hummed louder until I'd finished. The only toilet paper there was laid sideways and unrolled across the floor, which'd probably at some point also been white.

I stuck my foot through the hole to pull the door back and exhaled. Colt was crouched over his heels, tossing stones out into the parking lot. He stood once he realized I was behind him.

"I was guarding the door," he said.

"Thanks."

I walked toward the entrance of the store. He followed.

"Hey," he said.

I turned around.

"What'd you say your name was?" he said.

He pushed his hair back from his face. It caught in his eyebrow ring.

"I just forgot," he said.

"I didn't tell it to you."

I turned back around. He ran in front of me and blocked the door, either smiling or grimacing. I couldn't tell which.

"Tell me," he said. "You know mine."

"Could you move, please?" I said.

He didn't.

"It's Julia," I said.

"Julia," he repeated.

Then he turned inside, went back to his fridge. I walked to the counter, dumped some change from a plastic sandwich bag on top of the scratch tickets, and asked the old man for a jelly doughnut.

. . .

Outside the gas station, I sat on the curb licking every last trace of powder and purple goo from my fingers. It was the first thing I'd eaten all day. I could have eaten seventeen more.

"Julia."

I turned sideways, looking way, way up to the spotty stubble beneath Colt's chin. He held out a can of Sprite.

"Wash down that doughnut," he said.

I didn't move.

"Take it. It's on me. Well, the gas station. Which way are you going?"

I pointed.

"I could drive you," he said.

A tornado of dust and cigarette pack cellophane blew up in front of us, then settled back down as fast as it had started.

"I mean, some of the way," said Colt.

I cracked the can and sipped.

"Are you going somewhere?" I asked.

"I wasn't."

"Are you going to kill me?"

He made that weird face again.

"Do chickens fly?" he said.

||

· · ·

FARMS ROLLED OUT like sleeping bags on both sides of the road. Every time we passed sheep, I'd say, Sheep. Every time we passed cows, Colt said, Milk.

"Is this your car?" I asked him.

"Is now," Colt answered.

"Did you tell your boss you were leaving?"

"He's my grandpa."

"Did you tell your grandpa you were leaving?"

"He'll see I'm not there."

He picked some crust from around his eyebrow ring, wiped it on his shirt.

"Do you have a grandpa?" he asked.

"Yes," I said.

"Okay. And, what are you doing in my car right now?"

"You offered me a ride?"

"But, what are you doing? Where are you going?"

I pointed at some horses coming up on the left.

"Horses," I said.

It was quiet for a moment.

"What about allergies? Do you have one of those?"

"I don't think I do."

"You should know if you have an allergy."

"Well, I don't know."

"Can you eat peanut butter?"

"Yes."

"Can you walk up to pretty much any kind of flower and smell it?"

"I think so."

He nodded his head as if there were music playing, which there wasn't. Drummed his hands on the steering wheel.

"Do you smoke cigarettes?" he said.

"No."

"Me, neither," he said. "Not for real."

. . .

Hours passed. The sun went down. The forests on either side of us grew thicker, and the roads turned rocky and began to wind more and more. There were no houses or streetlights for miles. No McDonald's or pit stops. Just headlights and black road, and some growing car sickness. I thought of all the times I'd been told there was nothing more dangerous than a teenage boy. Except, of course, a teenage boy with a car. Yet here I was. Alone in the middle of nowhere with both.

Then the turn signal began to click. Colt pulled to the side. He turned off the ignition and turned toward me. Mouth agape, a black hole, hair falling over his eyes. He looked like a frightening muppet. I held my breath, holding the seat belt buckle.

"Gotta piss," he said.

He opened his door and jumped out. I let go. Glanced up at the rear-view mirror. At the back end of the car, he faced the ditch and unzipped. I looked away, out at the road ahead curving sharply out of sight. *They can't all be bad*, I thought. Maybe he's a nice boy.

Then a sudden smack against the window beside me. Colt had both hands pressed to the glass. I screamed. He screamed back.

"Please don't," I shouted, hitting the lock on the door.

"You don't," he shouted back.

I struggled with the buckle. Colt laughed.

"Don't be scared," he said. "Be normal. I just wanted to tell you something."

I moved over to the middle of the car. Locked the driver's door, too. Colt had backed away now, was standing in the ditch. He bent slightly to wave at me through the window.

"If I wanted to hurt you I would have opened the back doors by now."

I held my beating heart with one hand. Rolled the window down a crack with the other.

"Did you go?" I said.

"Yes."

I rolled it down a little more.

"So, let's go," I said.

"Come see this first."

"See what? It's dark."

"Just come."

I waited. Then, finally, unlocked and opened the door.

"There's probably, like, wolves or coyotes, or witches out here, watching us right now," I said.

"I'm not afraid of animals," said Colt. "Or witches."

He held out his hand. I took it, and he helped me down into the ditch beside him.

"This way," he said, leading me around to the back of the car.

"You want to show me your piss puddle?"

"No."

Then he turned around and grabbed hold of my forearms. Was trying to pull me onto the road. I screamed and pulled back.

"What are you doing?" I shouted. "You gonna throw me in front of a truck?"

"No, of course not. That would be morbidly insane."

Headlights lit the trees as a car towing a trailer sped around the curve. I pulled back harder, and we both fell into the damp ditch.

"See?" I said.

"See what?"

I stood, wiping the dirt from my backside.

"I better not have landed in your piss puddle."

He stood up, too, then looked both ways and ran out to the centre of the road on his own.

"Okay, come," he said.

"No."

"Come see," he said.

I stood there for a long time, it seemed. Waiting for something to change. Nothing changed. Eventually, I took one step onto the road. Once I'd done that, he ran back over to me, grabbed my hand, and pulled me farther out.

"Let me go," I said.

"Just look, Jules."

Dark was pressing from all sides but up. So I looked up. A pool of Milky Way beamed between the treetops, orange, yellow, and white like the end of a bowl of marshmallow cereal. I reached up my other hand instinctively, like I could touch it.

"Wondrous, right?" said Colt.

A horn blared and headlights flooded the road again. Still holding me, he hurled us both back into the ditch. We fell forward onto our hands and knees, and just as fast as it had appeared, the vehicle was gone. I pushed myself up, went straight for the passenger door.

"Don't call me Jules," I said.

III

....

COLT PROMISED I could trust him not to smother me with my own backpack if I fell asleep. I didn't believe him, but crawled into the back seat anyway. Stuffed one of my shirts, the thickest, warmest flannel one, beneath my head like a pillow. At times I'd wake up, from a muscle cramp, or the noises in my dreams, and expect to find myself upside down, limbs crushed, in a wreck off the side of a cliff. But there he'd be. All peaceful looking with one hand resting on the wheel, the other flicking a lighter. And, pretty quickly, I'd fall back to sleep.

IV

. . . .

AT DAWN I woke alone, aslope in the back seat. I sat up and looked out the window. Behind the car, in a small dirt lot surrounded by tall pine trees, was a trading post. I opened the door and climbed out, holding my backpack tight to my chest. Walked round to the front end of the car, parked crooked, and found one wheel stuck in a pothole. Colt emerged from the shop carrying two steaming paper cups.

"Jules," he called out, "hot chocolate."

He started jogging, keeping his arms as steady as possible while spitting hair away from his face. He still looked like a muppet. Though much less sinister in the morning light. I dropped my backpack onto the red, rusted hood and pulled out my map.

"Which way do we need to go?" he said.

I traced a line with my pinky finger. Colt leaned closer.

"This isn't a good map," he said.

"What do you mean, isn't a good map?" I said. "It shows us where we started. It shows us where to go."

"Stuff's missing."

"What stuff?"

He stuck his finger on a space marked with an X. "The whole town of Markstay should go here."

"It's a good map," I said.

He took a sip of his hot chocolate.

"Okay," he said. "I believe you."

I looked out to the road, then back down at the map.

"So, left from here, then follow the road beside this highway until we pass a lake."

I folded it back up and shoved it into my backpack. Colt handed me the second hot chocolate, then pulled himself up onto the hood. He patted the space next to him. I climbed up. The sun was rising over the pine trees, quickly warming the fresh air. Birds chirped. For a moment, the space around us felt serene.

"You know how to drive?" he said.

"Nope," I replied.

"Ready to learn?"

He elbowed me. I shifted toward the edge of the car.

"It's easy," he said. "I'll be your instructor."

"I don't think so," I said.

He slid from the hood, walked around to the passenger side, opened the door, and leaned against it. Then he sipped his hot chocolate, loudly, while staring at me. I stared back and blew the steam from mine.

"I've never driven in my life," I said.

"Have you ever ridden a grocery cart?"

"What?"

"It's no different. Don't be a chicken's pussy."

Then he reached across the seat and laid on the horn. Birds flew up from a nearby bush.

"Hey," I snapped. "People are sleeping."

"What people? The tree people?"

I climbed down from the hood and opened the driver's side door. He smiled, sat down in the passenger seat. I sat down in the driver's. Handed him my cup.

"Hold this," I said and started the car.

"Reverse," he said.

I pressed the gas. We lurched forward as the bumper bounced hard off the ground. Hot chocolate splashed onto the dash.

"Good work," he said. "You got us out of that hole just fine."

• • •

We drove down a narrow two-lane road with no other vehicles in sight. Colt told me when to speed up and slow down while he rested his head in his palm against the window, my flannel shirt now pulled up to his chin like a blanket. *This is okay*, I thought. It was almost like riding a grocery cart. I glanced over at Colt to tell him that, but his eyes were closed.

"Hey," I said.

He didn't answer. In the rear-view, a truck in the distance was gaining speed.

"Wake up," I said, louder.

The truck honked. His eyes stayed closed.

"Wake up!" I yelled, reaching to swat his shoulder, and in doing so, I swerved to the side of the road. The truck honked again. I grabbed the wheel with both hands and swerved in the other direction. The truck laid on the horn until I managed to straighten out, then it overtook us. As it passed the

driver flipped the bird, clearly mouthing many insults behind
his window. Once the truck was well ahead, I slowed the car to
a stop. Colt was still asleep. I shook him, hard.

"Colt," I yelled. "Get up. I'm not driving."

He moaned and shouldered me away. I shook him again.

"Just ignore him," he said. "People can be jerks."

I unbuckled my seatbelt and opened the door. Another car
honked as it approached from behind, and I pulled the door
shut. We were still in the middle of the lane. Once the car
had passed, I looked out the back window. Seeing no cars, I
climbed out and went around to Colt's side. Opened his door.
He fell sideways.

"Hey," he said, "can't a guy have a nap?"

"A guy can choose a better time to nap," I said. "Like when
he's not supposed to be the instructor."

He sighed, unbuckling his seatbelt.

"Fine," he said and stood from the car. "Switch."

. . .

A small blue sign on a tilted pole read *Baby Lake*. We pulled
over and tramped out into the trees. I told Colt to wait back so
I could find a place to squat. He walked out of sight, then once
my shorts were down, began to throw pebbles from wherever
it was he was hiding. After I'd yanked them back up, we hiked
a bit farther until we came to a dock leading out to the small
lake so still it was almost a perfect mirror. Colt immediately
stripped to his boxers and jumped in, shattering the illusion
while he dog-paddled around.

"Watch this," he shouted, then plugged his nose and dove
under, raising his bony legs up in a handstand that he quickly

fell out of. I took off my socks and shoes. Both smelled like
pickles.

"Did you see? One-handed," he said, spitting water.

"I saw."

He swam up to the dock.

"Belly flop contest," he said.

"Let's just call you the winner."

Then I sat down and dipped my feet in. He splashed water
up at my face.

"Come on," he shouted. "Flop that fucking belly."

"Go drown," I said, kicking water back at his face. He sputtered and shook out his hair. It reached far past his shoulders
when wet.

"Why aren't you coming in?" he said. "It's rejuvenative."

"I don't have a bathing suit."

"Aren't you wearing underpants?"

"Underpants are underpants," I said.

"Underpants are also bathing suits."

"They're my only ones."

"So jump in and wash them," said Colt. "That's what I'm
doing."

He somersaulted, then swam up to the dock and hung off
the end.

"Don't look," I said.

"I'm not."

"Close your eyes."

He squeezed his eyes shut. I waited, watching to see if he'd
peek. When he didn't, I quickly undressed to my underwear
and slipped in beside him, holding on to the edge of the dock.
The water was warm. He opened his eyes, then cheered, then
swam around me, spastic. I let go and floated on my back.

Above us, giant birds of prey circled, like the twins back home, snorkelling naked in their kiddie pool. I waited for them to drop straight for my stomach. Fighting each other with their talons like I was the last chocolate popsicle in the freezer.

V

. . .

AFTERNOON, WE PULLED into a town called Emo, and I was about ready to eat my own hands. We found a diner, sat in a sticky brown booth, and picked at a cherry Danish. I asked Colt how old he was, guessing sixteen. Seventeen, tops.

"Eighteen."

"Me, too," I responded.

He nodded.

"Sure. Okay. So are you ready to tell me where we're going?"

I licked a fleck of sugar off my wrist. I knew I'd eventually have to tell him, or else tell him to go back to his grandpa. But I didn't want to have to choose right then. I wanted to eat a cherry Danish.

"Is it a secret?" he asked. "'Cause I can keep a secret."

"How do I know that?"

"Come on. I've driven you all this way. I bought you that pastry."

"You basically kidnapped me."

"Are you going to find someone?"

"No."

"Who was supposed to be dead but it turns out they're alive?"

The lady in the booth in front of ours turned around in her seat.

"No one's dead. I don't think."

"But you want them dead?"

I didn't respond. Then I shrugged.

Colt leaned forward across the table, cheese he apparently didn't care about hemmed in the corner of his lips.

"Julia, are you a killer?" he said.

I smiled. Picked off another piece of Danish and dropped it into my mouth. Colt pounded the table.

"Damn it, Julia," he said. "Tell me what's going on. Please."

"I'm looking for a place. Called Egg Island. It's like, the subarctic."

A chair leg screeched across the floor as a man at a nearby table started coughing, pounding his hard, rounded chest. His bald head turning red.

"He's fine," said Colt. "What's in Egg Island?"

The man's sharp inhales turned to whistles. His wife stood and began slapping him on the back.

"I think he's really choking," I said.

Colt snapped his fingers at me. The woman switched position to stand in front of the man, gave him one hard punch to the stomach. A piece of pink something like a small organ shot from his throat and hit her in the chest. He gasped, regaining his own pinkish hue. Then took a drink of water and dabbed his neck and head with a napkin, while his wife rubbed an ice cube against her blouse. I looked at Colt, frowning back at me.

"Well?" he said.

"It's not really what's in it. More what's above."

Colt looked upward, slowly. Then back at me.

"It's one of the only places on Earth where you can see one," I said.

"One of what?"

"The holes. Like, to the other side."

"Like a volcano hole? That opens to hell? An arctic hell?"

"Subarctic. And no, because it's up in the sky."

He blinked.

"So it's one of those ozone holes they're always talking about. You wanna go see an ozone hole?"

"It might technically be in the ozone."

He reached across the table and tore off a piece of my Danish.

"Hey," I said.

"And this sky volcano in the ozone, it's above Egg Island," he said, popping the piece into his mouth.

"It's not a volcano. It's like, the rip in your jeans."

"It got caught on a piece of metal fence at the dump?"

"I don't know. Maybe. Anyway, through it, you see on to the next place. At least, that's what I was told," I said.

"By who?"

I looked over again at the woman and the choking man. Both their jaws back wrapped around triple-decker sandwiches, as if nothing had happened. No one'd nearly died that day.

"Some books. There are drawings of it, in books," I said.

"What's it look like?"

"Well, in some drawings it looks kind of green. Like the inside of a computer, or something. But in others it's more yellow. Or golden. Ish."

He sucked his fingers.

"Has anyone else ever been there?"

"Someone had to see it to draw the pictures."

"And that's it?" he said.

"I guess so."

"So you're looking for a rip in the sky. That was an accident, but kind of looks cool."

"Sure."

"And that you can see another world through?"

I nodded.

He sat up straight. Brushed the hair from his face. Clasped his hands together and placed them neatly on the table.

"You wanna split a burger?" he said.

"Really?" I said.

"This dainty Danish stuff ain't cutting it."

"Do you have money for a burger?" I asked him.

He pulled some bills and change from his front pocket, placed it on the table, and started to count.

"How much do you have?" he asked me.

I dug to the bottom of my backpack and pulled out the plastic bag of coins.

"There's not much in there," he said.

"It was my whole life savings."

"We're gonna need more money if we're going to make it all the way to the subarctic and back."

He spun a dime on the table, then clapped his hand over it.

"Wait," he said. "Are we coming back?"

"We?"

"You and me."

"Colt, we need to figure out how to get more money."

•   •   •   •

I left to use the washroom, and when I'd returned, Colt and all of our belongings had disappeared from the booth. All that remained were two cups, a small plate of crumbs, and a bill. I looked out the window to the parking lot. The car was gone, too. I backed up against the washroom door and scanned the restaurant for the waitress. She stood leaning against the doorway to the kitchen, her back to the tables, chatting with the cooks. I walked quickly across the tarnished tiles, trying not to squeak my sneakers. Then, through the glass door and out to the lot, where I ducked from view behind a van. I called out Colt's name in a whisper, as if he were standing on the other side of the van, then peeked around it at the diner window. Saw only my own head in the reflection of the parking lot. So I looked forward and ran. Across the road and down the sidewalk opposite, past a woman pulling a wagon full of groceries, a baby squatted amongst them. Then a group of at least five older kids who must have been on their lunch break, hanging outside a convenience store drinking gigantic neon slushies. I slowed down to catch my breath and searched, frantic, for any sign of the tall, dark-haired crazy person I'd most recently been travelling with.

"Jules."

I spun around. Then spotted him, knelt beside a dog tied to a parking sign a few shops down the street.

"What the hell?" I called out.

"It's a dog," he called back.

I walked over to him.

"So, here's the plan," he said.

"Did we just run out on that bill?"

"We're gonna go stroll around this town, or village, or hamlet, whatever it is, and panhandle for some extra cash. Shouldn't be too hard since you're a girl."

"Where's the car?"

"Pet the dog for good luck."

The dog arfed. I gave him a pat.

"Let's go," Colt said.

. . .

We continued along the main street until we reached the lot of a large farm supply store, out front of which many pickups and four-by-fours were parked. The air tasted like dust and manure.

"You think your grandpa's worried?" I asked Colt.

"Probably," he said, stooping to pick up a flattened coffee cup. Then he squatted down on a cement parking bumper, moulded the cup back into shape, and held it up to me.

"Here," he said.

"Ew," I replied.

"Just go over there and stick your arm out when someone passes by."

I looked at the cup, the lip of which had been gnawed thin.

"Take it," he said, his eyes on three women walking toward us. "We're about to miss out on a trio of perfectly good moms."

So I took the stupid cup, holding it with my thumb and forefinger, and walked toward the women.

"Hi," I breathed.

"Excuse us," one replied, bowing her purple sun hat as they walked past. I turned back to Colt. He shook his head.

"More slumpy," he said. "Like you're really desperate."

"I am desperate."

"Then look like it. Get down on the ground."

I squatted down and placed the cup between my feet. The next person to approach was a very tall man wearing a cowboy hat.

"Hi," I breathed, again.

He stopped, then came toward me.

"Yes?" he said, his voice like Elvis Presley's.

Looking up at him, I shielded my brow from the sun. His own face was almost entirely concealed by the brim of his hat.

"Hello, sir," I said, more clearly this time.

"Yes?" he repeated.

Behind me, Colt coughed.

"I was hoping you could help me with something," I said.

"Help you with what?" he said.

"We, I mean, I, need some assistance."

He glanced down at the cup.

"Assistance?"

I looked over my shoulder at Colt. He sighed, stood from the bumper, and walked over to where I was squatted.

"Apologies, sir," he said. "Please forgive my sister. She hasn't had it easy."

"How come I don't recognize you kids?" the man said.

"We're not from this beautiful whistle stop," said Colt.

"Where you from?"

"A faraway land. A cold, unfrequented place. Called Egg Island."

"That sounds made up."

"It's not," said Colt.

"How come I never heard of it?"

"Maybe you don't know every place in the whole world."

The man began to walk away.

"Wait," I called after him. "Please help us."

He paused. Then turned back. Cowboy hat pivoting between us.

"And what's wrong with her?" the man asked Colt.

"Well, first of all, she was a drug baby," he said.

"All right," said the man. "You kids really gotta go this far? For your wacky weed and your booze? And your Mary Jane? Bothering nice people in the streets and making up awful pity stories? For cash?"

"It's true," Colt started, but the man held up a finger.

"Because you know, there's people out there who got real troubles, like the kind you're saying. And the Lord don't look too kindly on folks who go around abusing the goodwill of other folks."

"Sir, really. We aren't looking to buy any wacky weed. The truth is, we're just a starving orphan and a drug baby. We hate booze and Mary Jane."

I rolled my eyes. The man hitched his pants with his thumbs.

"Tell you what," he said. "I got a couple sandwiches over there in the truck my wife packed up. Tuna, whole wheat. You get it. I tell her I'm not too fussy about it all, but she insists, on account of my arteries and whatnot. You take those, and that way I know you two ain't spending my hard-earned dollars, and the hard-earned dollars of the good people of this town, on no wacky weed or alcohol or booze or nothing. Plus, wife'll think I ate them up instead of a cheeseburger and fries, and she'll be happy enough not to bug me too much over supper."

I looked at Colt. He looked more desperate than a seagull.

"Whole wheat, though?" he said.

I stood up tall. Nudged him to the side.

"Thank you, sir," I enunciated. "How we would love some tuna on whole wheat bread."

We ate our sandwiches on the curb, coffee cup at my feet, which a few more people were nice enough to toss some coins into. Colt'd finished his in a few bites, so I offered him half of mine and basically had to feed it to him to get him to take it. Afterward, hunched over my knees, I played with my shoelaces. I felt like the snot of a crusted-up tissue in my dirty clothes, my white sneakers looking like they'd been rolled through a composter. Colt counted the change in the cup.

"There's almost fifteen bucks in here," he said. "You think we should go give it to that waitress?"

"I'm depressed," I said.

He placed his hand on the back of my head, finger-combed the knots of my greasy hair.

"You're okay," he said.

VI

· · · ·

SOMEWHERE BETWEEN THE town of Emo and nowhere, the sun began to go down behind a green hill. Pink spread like a sheet across the sky. All I wanted in that moment was to sleep in a real bedroom, with posters on the walls and china dolls and baby junk on shelves. Colt asked me if I was homesick. But I told him no. "For starters," I said, "I have these two little brothers, Michael and Zen, four-year-olds. They're twins. They almost never wear clothes, and they eat their cereal together out of a dog food bowl, and while it doesn't technically affect me, it hurts me to watch them like that. Like they're developing backward, or something. And they almost never take baths because they only like taking baths together, and Mom's been trying to wean them off of that, because all they do is bark and splash water all over the place and chew on the curtain and leave her with a flood to clean up afterward, which always makes her cry, or yell. And really, I'm afraid she's going to kill herself. Or otherwise go, for good, too. Because she's in love with a woman named Joan who she does swimming classes with, and Dad, well, he would just say there's no purpose to something like love, anyway. Or swimming classes. That when the end comes, it won't matter who has the strongest backstroke. And maybe he's not wrong. But still. Everyone will have disappeared, no hints, no money, and probably they'll just never look back. And I'll be stuck taking care of the twins while my mind wastes away until it's about as sharp as mashed potatoes."

"Would you care if I told you we were lost right now?" Colt asked.

"I guess not," I said.

VII

WE TURNED ONTO a forested dirt road marked by a large sign that read *WELCOME TO BLIND BAT PARK* between a cartoon bat and a mosquito of the same size. After following the road another half mile, we pulled up to a shack with *Visitor Information* painted across the door.

Inside, a tiny old woman in a giant raincoat sat behind the counter fiddling with a radio. Some jazz station faded in and out of static. Colt asked her if we could park in a tenting spot, just for the night.

"Thirty," she said.

"Okay. But we don't exactly have thirty dollars," Colt responded.

"How much you got, exactly?"

"Like, half of that."

She snorted.

"We'll be out by dawn" he said.

She looked me up and down. I slapped a mosquito on my thigh, leaving a big bloody smudge.

"You gotta be eighteen to rent a campsite," the woman said.

"I am eighteen," Colt said.

"How old's she?"

"Also eighteen," I said.

"I can't let you kids stay here for free. And from the look of you both, I oughta be calling social services."

I slapped another mosquito, this time on my neck.

"Let's just go," I said to Colt.

"We have fifteen dollars, almost," he continued. "It's in a cup. But it still works."

Then I swatted a big one feasting on his shoulder. The old lady examined us. Back and forth, up and down. "For Pete's sake," she said, painfully pushing herself up from her wooden chair. Snorting and muttering to herself, she bustled around the shack like a rodent, gathering a pile of necessities: repellent, four bottles of water, a package of cold hot dogs.

"I think she's an angel," Colt whispered.

"Or the ghost of one," I replied.

•   •   •

The spot was just big enough for the car and some stumps that circled a tiny fire pit. We turned the headlights on and sprayed each other down. Colt started a fire while I used a rock to wrench the top off a can of beans. Bats dove about the trees above us, chirping creepy bat tunes. It was just like we were playing house.

"How lost are we, really?" I said to Colt.

"Well, I don't know where we are, really," he said.

A loon called from the lake. The pine needles in the fire burst like caps from a cap gun. *If you're part of the family, you'll know*, Dad'd told me. *And when you're ready, you'll also know.*

Because your legs will just start walking. Like you're being pushed from the wrong magnet and pulled to the right.

I coughed from the smoke.

"It's that weird map," said Colt, coughing, too. "I told you, stuff's missing."

"We'll figure it out," I said. "It's not like no one in the world has ever been lost before."

Colt bent closer to his small flame and started blowing.

"At least we have hot dogs," he said.

And once the flame grew, we roasted them from the tips of two long sticks. They whistled and bubbled with sweat. At one point, Colt turned to me, smiling, the whites of his teeth aglow in the dim light. Pieces of chewed-up beige wiener stuck in the gaps.

"What the hell are you smiling at?" I said.

"You," he said. "You're my best friend."

"I'm your only friend," I said.

"An equally important status."

• • •

We woke to a loud crash against the back end of the car. I shot up in the back seat. Colt covered his head with my flannel that he'd been snuggling as the car shook, then shook again. All the air in my lungs seemed to plummet to my bowels. Colt was going shhh, and he reached around the front seat to hold my hand, as if holding hands would protect us from whichever forest witch had finally come to devour our souls.

"Don't move," he said.

I sat up and looked through the rear windshield.

"I can't see anything," I said. "It's too dark."

Another blow, this time to the door beside me. I slid over to the other side of the car. Colt shifted down as low in the seat as his long legs would allow, trying to fit himself into the space beneath the steering wheel. After a moment of stillness, I peeked over his seat to look out the front windshield. A small black bear pawed at our fire pit.

"It's just a bear," I said.

"Quiet," Colt hissed.

"Relax. He can probably smell fear or whatever."

I climbed between the front seats and got into the passenger side.

"What the hell are you doing?" he screeched up at me.

"Scaring him away."

I started the engine, and the car lights turned up. The bear stumbled backward in confusion.

"He's cute," I said.

"Fuck you, he's cute," Colt said. "Bears kill people. They're murderers."

The bear shook his head and snorted, struggling to remove the plastic hot dog wrapper that had gotten stuck to its snout.

I laid on the horn. The bear froze. Then wiggled its big butt off into a bush.

"Is he gone?" Colt said.

"He's gone."

Colt didn't move.

"You can come out now," I said.

"I can't."

"Are you stuck?"

"No."

"What's the matter?"

"There's been an accident," he whispered.

VIII

· · · · · ·

THE SECOND IT was morning, we walked down to the lake. Colt waded in up to his knees, repeatedly dunking, then sniffing, then dunking his jeans in the water again. I dug my toes into the cold mud of the beach.

"It's okay," I said. "It happens to the best of us."

"When was the last time you peed your pants?" he said.

"Like, in gym."

He twisted the jeans until they wouldn't twist anymore.

"What grade was that?"

"One."

"Don't tell anybody. This is between you and me."

"Who would I tell? The ghost lady back there? She's probably wearing a diaper herself."

He waded out farther, up to his ribs. Twisted around at the waist like he was doing a little dance. Then traipsed back to shore looking miserable, boxers clinging to his pale legs. His whole body was goose-bumped.

"You'll dry off in no time," I said.

He pulled at his underpants.

"You can't understand," he said.

I wrapped the flannel around his shoulders, gave them a good rub. Walking back from the lake, we passed the visitor hut, where the old woman was sitting outside on a royal-blue beach chair. Upon seeing us, she immediately turned on her scowl.

"Good morning," I said to her. "Did you know you have bears?"

"Of course we have bears. What happened to him?"

She nodded at Colt, holding the shirt together at his throat with one hand.

"Just needed a bath," I said.

She grunted.

"Actually," he said to the woman. "We were hoping we could ask one more favour. Then I promise we'll be gone. For all of eternity."

I looked at him. "What favour?"

"Do you have a phone?" he asked the woman.

"Who do you need to call?" I asked him.

"Do you have a phone?" he said again.

She stood from her chair like she was rising from her grave. Hobbled toward the door.

"You come with me," she said to Colt, waving him inside. He went ahead, and I followed, uninvited.

Through the back of the store was a small office. Pushed against the mouldy plywood hammered into the wall was an old wooden desk, a computer, a fax machine, and a telephone all set on top. About half a dozen taxidermied animal heads were propped around the floor.

"Sit," she ordered, then picked up the receiver. Listened, pressed a button, listened again. Then handed it over to Colt.

He wheeled back the swivel chair in front of the desk and sat down. I locked eyes with a buck missing one half of his antlers. Everything was quiet while Colt punched the numbers.

"Hi," he said.

Audible hollering from the other end.

"I'm okay," said Colt. "It's okay."

I could hear curses amongst the babble. Colt rubbed his forehead and blinked quickly. I acted like I was busy admiring the peeling brown wallpaper. He cupped the receiver and turned his back to me.

"Please don't do that," I heard him say. "Please." Then, "Are my ants okay? No. But I do care about them."

Then a pause on both ends.

"Miss you, too. Love you, too," he said.

. . .

We sat in the car with the doors open, map spread across the dashboard. Colt tried to act extra enthusiastic about being lost and hungry and low on gas while wearing clothes that smelled like fish.

"You don't have to act tough," I said.

"I am tough," he replied.

I studied the map, the route forward and the route back to where we began. I also studied a red dot in neither of those directions called Vermilion Bay.

"Here," I said, pointing to the dot. "We'll get gas and food. I'll beg for more money."

"Isn't that out of the way?"

"It might be our only shot for a while. Look at all this empty space. There can't be any human life there. At least, not the kind we'd want to run into."

Colt shrugged and started the car, turned the volume up on the static coming from the radio. Something familiar was trying to break through. Sounded like "Tiny Dancer." I looked over at the shack, where the woman was glowering at us through a dirty window. We pulled the car doors shut.

"Wave goodbye to the angel," I said.

The angel didn't wave back.

IX

· · · ·

VERMILION BAY AND its surrounding area apparently had a population of one thousand people, but I couldn't see a single living being anywhere. We pulled up to a restaurant with one ancient gas pump we weren't even certain worked, and Colt climbed out to give it a shot. The meter on the dash went up two notches. He stopped pumping. The air was cool, and the sky was grey.

Inside the restaurant, a man as old as the gas pump outside was propped up in a booth with his head against the window, either sleeping or dead, and a young woman in overalls and a pink cardigan leaned against a till counter lined with pies. Her gold nametag read *Peggs*. She looked up at us from her copy of *The Bridges of Madison County*.

"Hi there," I said, "I'm here to inquire about your pies?"

Peggs placed a finger on the line she was reading.

"Grab a table, I'll be right over."

Colt stepped up to the counter and placed the coffee cup of coins on top.

"Can I give you this for the gas?" he asked.

Peggs looked down at the cup.

"What's this?" she said.

"Cash money," said Colt.

"How much'd the meter run?"

"A couple of ticks on the clock thing," he said.

She placed the book opened face down on the counter, then picked up the cup. Tipped it slightly to count the coins at the bottom.

"Have a seat at that table. I'll get you a receipt."

So we sat, once again, across from one another in a sticky diner booth. Both of us looked down at our hands, which we both held clasped on our laps. Then we ping-ponged glances at one another. It was a good silence. I wanted it to last. It couldn't last.

"What else do you think we'll find there?" Colt asked.

Peggs appeared beside us and placed two sets of cutlery on the table.

"We're not ordering food," I told her.

"Coke or Sprite?" she said.

"We don't have enough money for anything, ma'am," said Colt.

"Ma'am? You can give me a hand with some boxes after."

I nodded at Colt. He shrugged.

"Coke or Sprite?" she asked again.

"I suppose Sprite," said Colt. "Times two. Thanks. Miss."

Peggs disappeared through a swinging kitchen door. I unrolled the cutlery sets, placed each piece neatly atop its napkin, and slid a set over to Colt. Rain had started splattering against the window. The car and gas pump outside appeared smudgy through the glass, like a smudged-up pencil drawing. Colt yawned and unrolled his napkin.

"Well?" he said.

"She's nice," I replied.

"Anything up there other than a giant hole?"

I tried to imagine it. A group of people in matching orange snowsuits, standing together in a circle like a bunch of eager pylons, waiting to be sucked up to their next life, their happy life, beneath the green or yellow or goldenish eye of their maker. Or just one man, all alone. Clinging to life, claiming to know the truth.

"Probably some ice fishing huts," I said.

Peggs reappeared carrying a tray topped with two fizzing plastic cups and two face-sized slices of blueberry pie. Colt straightened as she set the food on the table. Looked at the pie, at me, at Peggs, who was smiling back down at him.

"Two Sprites," she said, before taking her tray back to the counter, back to her book. Colt picked up his fork and knife.

"Can you believe this?" he said, carving out his first perfect triangular fragment.

I leaned in close and sniffed it.

"It's not a flower," he said.

I took up my own fork and stabbed a hole directly in the centre.

"Does it scare you?" said Colt.

"Ice? Or pie?"

"Whatever's up there. What if it's carcinogenic?"

I dug out the guts and lifted them to my mouth.

"Or proof," I said.

"Proof of what?"

"That everything else is actually meaningless."

Colt carved another bite.

"You know," he said, chewing, "if you think about it, the dinosaurs were here for like, millions of years, just stomping around, not doing anything useful. We've been here for way less time than that, and look at everything we've done. We built all these cities. We invented cars, escalators. We even sent a man to the freaking moon."

"What does that have to do with anything?" I said.

He took another bite. Then set down his cutlery, wiped his mouth with his napkin, and took a long pull through his straw. Then looked straight at me and burped.

"Things can be meaningless and meaningful at the same time," he said.

I looked down at the crater I'd made in my pie. It wasn't enough. I needed the whole thing, and I needed it right away. So I dropped my fork on the table, tore the crust off with my fingers and ate it like that, while Colt continued to work through his slice as though it were a gift. Which it was. He was right. So we ate. And the only sounds between us from that point were teeth gnashing, and Chuck Berry, and silverware scraping scratched-up china plates.

. . .

We followed Peggs through a kitchen that had been collecting grease since the 1950s to a prep room in the back. Boxes upon boxes of books had been pushed against a wall, with sacks of potatoes and flour and crates full of indiscernible junk piled up in front of them. A tray of butter knives sat atop a steel table dented in the middle. I picked a nesting doll off the top of a pile, opened it. It was empty.

"What's all this stuff doing here?" I asked.

"If you don't mind moving that produce down to the cold room, that sure would save Jerry a lot of backache."

Colt picked up a box of cabbage.

"Watch your head," she said, before turning back through the kitchen.

I set the doll down on the table beside the knives. Colt ducked beneath a doorframe and plodded down the staircase. I picked out a rag from a plastic shopping bag, tipped over an empty milk crate, and began polishing the silverware.

"What's down there?" I called down to him. "Another dimension?"

"Nah," he said, re-emerging. "Just chainsaws, human scalps."

He lifted a bag of onions. I picked up a knife and ran my thumb along the dull serrations of the blade.

"Can I ask you something?" I said.

"You can ask me anything at all, whenever you want."

"What do you think you'd be doing if you weren't here right now?"

"Where else would I be?"

"Back home. What would you be doing if you were back home?"

He hoisted the onions up onto his shoulder, holding them steady with one hand.

"Opening boxes, probably. Jerky boxes. Stocking jerky."

"Other than that."

"Well, I also stock pop and stuff, as you know. My grandpa leaves me in full charge of the fridges."

"For fun. If you were having fun. Like, what'd you do before all of this?"

"Oh. I don't know. Skateboard. Make fires. Take care of the ants in my ant farm. You have to feed them, water them.

Make sure their house is the right temperature. I'm God to those little guys."

He shifted the bag to the other shoulder and shook out his arm.

"Right, so, why are you doing this, then? When you could be doing all those other things?" I asked him.

"Because," he said.

Then he turned around, went back through the portal. Outside, the rain was picking up. I could hear it against the roof. I looked at the knife in my hand, then very slowly ran the rag over it. Over and over. Erasing all the little watermarks, specks of rust.

"What are you doing?" Colt yelled.

I looked up. A leak had formed in the corner of the room. He dashed toward it from the top of the stairs, holding his hands out like a bowl.

"Get a pot or something," he shouted. "Save the books."

I scanned the room. There was an empty bucket beneath the metal table.

"I don't see anything," I lied. "I'll check the kitchen."

"Run," he said.

And I did. Through the kitchen, past Jerry hunched over the grill, then I slipped around the corner into a washroom the size of a broom closet. Locked the door, flipped down the lid, and sat on top. Read, *Pete is a blow job* etched above the toilet paper holder. I took a few deep breaths, but all I could think about were ants. Thousands and thousands of ants, working in never-ending circles of sand tunnels inside a glass box, worshipping Colt for all of their brief existences.

Colt banged on the door. Called my name. I looked around the washroom, as if there were anything in there that could help me make a decision about what to do next. And then I saw the window.

"Julia," he said. "Crisis averted. There was a bucket all along."

I stood on the toilet and pushed up the pane. He knocked again.

"You okay?" he said. "You having diarrhea?"

I heaved my body up, lifted myself out and into the cold rain. Then ran toward the car. Not wanting to look back to the window or the table where we sat. Not wanting to change my mind. In the back seat, my bag had unzipped and the contents spilled out onto the floor. Sweater, pads, crusty sock balls. Empty Thermos, dead Walkman. I quickly swept it all back inside. Then shut the door and began to walk. Stuck my thumb out to the road as a blue SUV glided toward me. Slow down, I told it. Slow down, slow down. It slowed down.

X
. . .

THE DRIVER'S NAME was Charles. He was probably thirty or forty, maybe even fifty years old.

"You must be cold," he said.

I wrapped the flannel around my shoulders like a towel. But it was wet, too. Everything was. I hadn't even zipped my backpack. I dug to the bottom to check that the map was there and still intact. He switched on the heater. It rustled the thick curls that hung around his face, and one wayward strand of grey danced straight upward like a charmed snake.

"How long were you waiting out there?" he said.

I opened my mouth to speak, but couldn't. So I closed it. The tires hissed against the wet road. Rain smacked against the windshield like a broom beating a dirty rug. I kept my eyes forward, avoiding the mirrors, afraid to see Colt's grandpa's car on the road behind us.

After some time, Charles said, "Not long?"

I nodded.

"Is there anyone who would want to know where you are right now?"

I shook my head no.

"Parents?" he said.

"None."

"Aunts or uncles?"

"I was born into a cult. I don't know which cult members are my blood relatives and which are just my cult relatives."

"Really?" said Charles.

"Yes."

It was quiet again. For a second.

"I don't really believe you," he said.

"No, you're right," I said. "I know who my blood relatives are. Some of them. We have the same triangle carved into the skin above our hearts. Like perfect little slices of pie."

"I feel like I should take you to the police station."

"You don't need to do that."

"Where is it you're even going?"

I searched the distance for a sign, any sign, of the place I was heading for. There was none.

"Do you have any allergies?" I said.

"If you're in trouble, you can tell me."

"Look," I started. Then stopped again. Each time I tried to speak, it felt as though I were running out of breath. "You seem like a really normal person," I said. "Maybe even kind of rich, considering how clean the floor of your car is. And all this digital stuff where the radio should be."

"That is a radio," he said.

"Point is, I know you probably think you need to help me. But all I really need help with is getting a little farther down this road."

Charles didn't respond. Instead, after a moment, he pressed a button that set the bright-blue screen on the radio aglow. Gentle classical music sounded through the speakers.

"Does your cult have a name?" he asked.

"Of course."

"What is it?"

"I'm not able to provide such information at this time," I said.

"Children of God? Heaven's Gate?"

"Perhaps," I said.

"Wow," he said. "It's probably a good thing you escaped, then."

"Yes. It is."

"I have a daughter," he continued. "About your age. She's going through a phase where she's afraid aliens will come in through her window at night. She wakes up sometimes screaming, claiming she's seen some radiant green light through the curtains."

I didn't respond.

"And then I have to sit there with her until she falls back asleep. It can take a while."

"Aliens aren't real," I said.

"There's a police station in the next town."

I picked up my backpack from between my feet, hugged it tight to my body, and placed my hand on the door handle.

"Okay," he said. "Relax. You don't have to jump out of the car."

But I kept my hand where it was. Because in the pocket of the door panel were two crumpled-up twenty-dollar bills. I thumbed one into my fist. Then thumbed the second into my fist, as well. Finally, a sign appeared for an upcoming rest stop.

"You can let me off there," I said, pointing at the sign with my other hand. "It's basically where I was going."

"A burger joint in the middle of nowhere?"

"Yes," I said.

"Didn't you just come from one of those?"

"It wasn't the right one."

· · ·

As we approached the rest stop, Charles slowed, turned into the drive, and pulled up close to the door.

"There's a payphone," he said, pointing through the window. "Take this and get some quarters."

He held out a folded bill. I took it in my empty hand, but didn't move from the car.

"Are you getting out?" he said.

"Yes," I said, still not moving.

"Are you sure I can't take you someplace else?"

I opened the door.

"I know you have a daughter," I said. "But what if I were some crazed, pollen and peanut-laced stabber person who was planning on robbing you and taking your car and abandoning you on the side of the road?"

He frowned. "Pollen?"

I opened the door. Stepped from the safe, warm car and back out into the rain.

"How would you ever know?" I said, before closing the door.

· · ·

Sitting at a cold metal table, a tray set in front of me, the greasy foil from a cheeseburger crushed into a tight ball, I chewed on the straw from my chocolate shake, the melting remains of which were now leaking through the bottom of the cardboard cup. A pile of dirty napkins. A country pop song playing too loud for comfort. Rows of tired families, their large camper vans parked outside, sunken into booth seats, picking at cold fries before packing themselves back up into their travelling homes. Charles had given me a fifty-dollar bill. I didn't get any quarters.

Eventually, the restaurant emptied, and the only employee left behind the counter was counting out her till. Half the lights turned off and the music cut out. The smell of old mop water and bleach overtook the smell of fryer oil.

"Closing in fifteen," a woman's voice echoed.

I pressed my forehead against the table. Moments later, she called out, louder. "Miss, we need to lock the doors."

I looked over to the counter where she stood leaning against a mop, her other hand on her hip.

"Are you talking to me?" I said.

"Well, I'm not talking to Andrew," she replied.

I stood, gathered my still-damp flannel and backpack, and slowly made my way to the exit, which she immediately locked behind me. Outside, the parking lot was completely dark and empty except for one vehicle, hers or Andrew's, I guessed. The rain had stopped, but the air was cold. I turned and looked back into the restaurant, hoping one of them might take pity and offer me a ride, or a roof. A hug, even. But the lights were out. No one in sight now. No one anywhere. I was alone. I walked around to the back of the restaurant, where two over-flowing Dumpsters stank beneath the stars. Across another smaller road was a motel, its vacancy sign half blown out, almost all of its windows dark.

XI

····

I TRIED THE door. Locked. So I tapped on the glass. Inside, a four-hundred-year-old-man in a security uniform slept in a chair behind the front desk. I knocked harder. He didn't budge. I cupped my hands against the glass. "Hello," I called. His head drooped downward. I took a few steps back, examined the length of the building. A long white strip of ten blue doors.

I went around to the back of the building, but couldn't see more than a few feet in front of me. So I took a few slow steps forward, as if testing water. The ground was swampy. It seeped through my sneakers. The curtains were shut in the first window, open in the next. A man and woman slept topless in bed, his arm around her torso, cupping her chest. I ducked down and crept forward. Counted the third, fourth, and fifth rooms, all with windows closed. At the sixth, the curtains were open. I looked inside. Though dark, it appeared to be vacant. The bed was made and there was no luggage or clothing, as far as I could see. I ran my index finger along the edges of the screen.

Then a light switched on at the end of the row. I dropped to the ground and shut my eyes, as if that would make me invisible. *I was a good kid*, I thought. I paid attention. I helped. And I didn't complain about it, either. Yet here I was. A hobo thief breaking into a creepy motel a million miles from home. The light turned off, and I opened my eyes again to pitch dark. Stood, pushed on the screen so it popped into the room, and pulled myself up through the window.

First, I slipped off my shoes. The carpet was rough beneath my wet socks. I touched the desk. The pen and pad of notepaper were labelled for a dentist's office. A laminated sheet of TV channels. Beneath the desk was a small mini fridge, inside of which were three Halloween-sized chocolate bars and a mini bottle of vodka with a broken seal. Beside the desk was a wardrobe, the top half a set of cupboard doors which opened to reveal a small television. I turned the volume knob all the way down before switching it on to a fuzzy Indian soap opera with subtitles. Then, to *Late Night*. I took the three chocolate bars, pulled my legs up onto the springy bed, and for a moment, forgot where I was, what I'd done. Whatever the hell mess I'd be in tomorrow. I was back in my room with my tiny TV. Just me and Conan hanging out, having a time of it in the middle of the night.

XII

I WOKE TO a chill draft around my neck, as though a phantom were breathing next to me. My body itchy beneath the stiff wool blanket. I pushed it off of myself and sat up on the bed. The television was still on, muted, a morning church service. People raising their hands to the ceiling. Then crying. Then applauding. I climbed out of bed, went to the washroom and splashed water on my face, used my finger like a toothbrush. Grabbed the small soap and shampoo from the shower, dropped them into my backpack with my new pen and dentistry stationery, then zipped up. The people on the screen were singing and dancing now. Clapping, waving their arms. Some still crying. I rocked back and forth a little, dancing with them for a moment, even though I couldn't hear their music. When it cut to commercial, I turned the television off. Went to the window and popped the screen again. Dropped the backpack out, and climbed after it into the brilliant new day.

"Morning, dipshit."

On a plastic patio chair fifteen feet away from the window sat a woman surrounded by a field of sunburned grass. She had enormous breasts and bleached hair cropped like a mental patient's. A long cigarette burned between her fingers and the steaming mug in her hand. A rifle leaned against her thigh.

"Sleep well?"

I stood up straight and pulled on the straps of my bag.

"Hah," she barked. "You think I wouldn't notice? Some punk breaking into one of my rooms?"

She took a loud, sucking sip of her coffee. I wanted to run.

"Don't even think about it," she said.

"What?"

"I got perfect aim."

I laughed, weak.

"What, you think I'm joking?" she said. She patted the gun. "The scope on this thing can peg a running deer six hundred yards away. Straight between the eyes. In the dark. I know it. I've done it."

"The guy at the front desk was asleep. I didn't know what to do," I said.

The woman coughed a loud hacking cough, then raised her elbow level to her chin to take a drag. Ash tumbled down the front of her chest, but she'd clearly stopped caring about things like that decades ago.

"You all alone, girly?"

"Mm," my voice cracked.

"What was that? Mm? What's that? What's a Mm?"

"I'm alone," I said.

"You sure?" She cocked the gun. "No boyfriend hiding anywhere, got the wrong idea in his head?"

I shook my head no. She took a long, slow pull off her cigarette and stubbed it out on the leg of her chair. Then heaved
herself up like she was weighted with elephant tusks and picked
up the gun by the barrel. I didn't move.

"Let's go," she said.

"Go where?" I asked.

She looked at me, sighed. "I gotta come over there and drag
you by the hair? Move."

She headed toward the front of the building. Far back in
the distance, directly in line with her chair, a black dot roosted
on a naked bush.

"I said move," she yelled back, without turning around.
I began to walk. She paused at the corner of the building. I
looked back at the bush. The dot was gone.

. . .

Her home was the tenth room of the motel. Same as the room
I'd slept in, but embellished. The bed dressed in a fleece blanket with a tiger face on it. Some fake flowers in a vase on the
desk, small elephant ornaments and decorative bowls propped
along the TV and nightstands. A bead curtain hung in front
of the washroom.

"Shut the damn door," she said. "You'll let in the wasps."

I stepped inside and shut the door.

"Open that," she said, pointing her gun at a miniature
fridge. I bent over and opened it. Inside was a pile of meats
wrapped in paper and twine.

"One from the top," she said, then with one hand, struck a
matchstick against a bible on the desk and lit the burner of a gas
hot plate. The flame erupted, blue. I backed up toward the door.

"How old, chiquita?"

"Eighteen."

"Hah," she barked. "I'm twenty-five."

She stepped in front of me, her massive form blocking out the light, and leaned the gun against the doorframe. The barrel knocked on the wood. Then she went back to her hot plate, forked margarine onto a pan. It sizzled up in large, brown bubbles.

"My next question was gonna be what are you doing breaking into my motel, but if that's how it's gonna go, me asking questions and you lying your answers back, guess I'll save my breath."

She unwrapped the meat, placed it on the pan.

"I am," I said again.

"You are what?"

"Eighteen."

The meat crackled and smoked.

"I said, and I'm twenty-five."

The smell began to overwhelm the room. I couldn't tell if it was good or bad. There was blood on her hands from handling the paper it had been wrapped in.

"It's a federal offence," she continued. "If you are eighteen, you're in mighty big trouble committing a federal offence. But I hear juvie's no walk in the park, either."

"I have money. I can pay for the room and go," I said.

She picked up an orange from a bowl of oranges tucked inside the television cupboard. Bit into the rind and peeled a chunk off with her teeth.

"Oh, you'll be paying," she said, spitting the rind into her palm. Then she turned her back to me, pushed back the beaded curtain, and leaned into the washroom. Turned around holding a small bucket and a metal mallet. I glanced at the gun.

"It isn't loaded," she said.

She pulled the chair from the desk and placed the bucket on the seat. Chewed the remaining peel off, then dropped the orange into the bucket. Proceeded to hammer it into juice.

"You wanna end up raped?" she said between breaths.

I shook my head no. She paused her grinding and looked up, pointing the dripping mallet at me.

"You don't know what sick asshole you might run into out there."

Smoke from the pan was filling the room. My eyes began to water.

"What is that?" I asked.

"Food."

"What kind of food?"

"Can't trust men," she said. Then she set the bucket on the floor and stood there holding the mallet in her hand, gripping and re-gripping it like a baseball bat. I looked to the window covered in old orange drapes, slightly translucent and stained with circles of bleach.

"All right," she said.

She pulled a shot glass from the TV stand. Set the mallet head down on a coaster and used the glass to scoop juice from the bucket. Handed it to me and waited.

"Don't be rude, kid," she said.

I looked down at the juice, then back at the woman, then at the mallet resting on the desk. I lifted the glass to my mouth, sipped. She reached forward and tilted my chin all the way up. I choked, coughed. Then she took the glass from me, dipped it into the bucket again, and took a drink herself.

"I got a daughter, too. She was your age once. Ran off on her own more than a few times. Thought she was Lynda Carter or some damn thing."

"Everyone has a daughter," I said.

"What was that?"

I shook my head as if I'd said nothing. She turned back to the pan, stabbed the meat with the fork, and lifted it onto a plate. Then, with a hunting knife she pulled out of a holster at her ankle, she cut a chunk and pushed it onto a second plate. Held it out to me.

"Eat," she said.

"What is it?" I asked.

"Liar and a picky eater?"

I took the plate. It looked almost like a pink leg of chicken. But not quite. She took a bite from her own plate, wheezed while she chewed.

"It's good," she confirmed.

I touched the meat with my middle finger, wishing Colt was there to pass it off to.

"Did you find her in the end?" I asked the woman.

She sucked her teeth.

"Eat your squirrel," she said.

XIII

BETWEEN THE STONES of the walkway that led to the office door, I dug in my fingernails and yanked out each wad of crabgrass. Bruises were forming beneath my kneecaps from kneeling on the cement. Red ants crawled from the cracks and nipped at my bare legs. The woman stood over me holding a garbage bag. I shielded my eyes and looked up at her.

"Do you have any pants?" I asked.

"Who do you think I am, the mall?"

A phone rang from inside the office.

"Finish this," she said, dropping the bag beside me. "Then we'll get started with the paint."

She went inside and stood over the desk. I sat back on my heels. Through the glass door, her broad torso looked like a whale underwater. I blinked, then looked out to the road, where a woolly black dot strutted down the centre line. I rubbed my eyes with the back of my arm. It disappeared.

She motioned for me to continue weeding with the phone pressed to her ear. I crawled forward, pulled another bunch,

and held it up for her to see. Then she turned her back to me
again. The phone cord stretched beyond the desk as she dug
through a filing cabinet behind it. I flicked an ant from my
thigh. Looked back out to the road. Then I stood, walked over
to the office door. Opened it a crack and leaned in. She looked
up at me and waved me back out. I made a drinking motion.
Her hulking chest heaved with a sigh, and she covered the telephone receiver.

"Go get some water from the sink. Two minutes. Straight
there and back."

Before the door shut behind me, she yelled.

"Wait."

I turned around.

"Hot tap's cold, cold tap's hot."

. . .

I counted down the row of blue doors until I reached hers at the
end. Pushing it open, I was once again slugged with the smell
of cooked roadkill. It just smelled bad now. I found a glass in
the TV cabinet, passed through the beaded curtain into the
washroom, and filled it from the sink. It tasted like licking
a metal pole. But I forced it and a second cup down anyway.
Then I stepped out of the washroom and stood there, in the
middle of her house. The gun was where she'd left it, leaned
against the doorframe. I wondered where she kept her bullets.
I tossed the glass onto the bed, walked over to the rifle. Picked
it up like I was picking up a baby, then held it, laid across
both hands. It was much heavier than I'd expected. The metal
along the barrel was warm from the trapped heat of the room.
I pointed it outward, at a mirror on the wall opposite me. I

looked like Dirty Harry, but with longer hair. Or the kid on the cover of the military school pamphlet. Placed my finger on the trigger and whispered, "Bang."

I fell backward onto the floor. The gun fell and fired again. The mirror had shattered. There were two bullet holes: one near the floor, one where the reflection of my mouth had just been. Ears ringing, arms limp, I pushed myself up. Grabbed my backpack and ran like hell.

XIV

· · · · · ·

I WALKED FOR what felt like several hours with a ringing in my ears before being picked up by a young couple driving a loud green truck, patches of rust lining the door handles and wheel arches. I tossed my bag onto the bed next to a large rucksack and three smaller duffel bags, then cramped into the back seat beside a girl with a tall nest of dreadlocks tied up on the top of her head with a yellow bandana. She had a silver nose ring and seven studs up the side of each ear. The driver drove well over the limit. Windows rolled down, the whipping air and engine noise drowned out the voice of the young woman up front, who was practically shouting back to us to be heard. Her feet were propped up on the dashboard as she painted her toenails baby blue, perfectly neat, despite the bumpy ride. She told us they'd been hitchhikers, too, once, and once made it all the way from Alaska to Toronto in the middle of February with nothing but their feet, thumbs, and ethical spirits.

"We were WWOOFing," she yelled.

I asked her what that meant.

"You don't know?" she yelled back.

"You don't know WWOOFing?" Dreadlocks echoed.

"Like, dogs?" I asked.

"Like, where you work on farms in exchange for food and shelter. That's how we survived our journey."

"You learn a lot about environmental preservation, too," Dreadlocks added.

"What?" I shouted.

"The environment," the young woman yelled.

"Like, dogs?" I said.

"It's literally magical," the young woman yelled again.

In the rear-view mirror, I could see the driver's glassy eyes fixed on the road ahead. After several moments, he still hadn't blinked.

"Where are you going now?" I shouted.

"Fargo," the young woman yelled.

"Fargo?"

"It's where Andy's family's from." She placed her hand on the driver's shoulder. "His mom lives in a home."

I looked at Andy again. No change.

"Does she like it there?" I shouted.

"What?" she shouted back.

"Does she like it?" I yelled, slower.

"The home?" the young woman shouted back. "Would you?"

I looked at Dreadlocks. She snorted. I shrugged. The young woman stuck her foot out the open window and wiggled her blue toes. Andy pulled off the highway, and we began driving down a long, thin road, chunks of concrete broken off along the sides of it. We passed a sign that read *Shoal Lake Reserve*, then farther down the road, rows of white and green houses shaped like Monopoly pieces. Some had small gardens, slanted porches, graffiti, and missing windows. We pulled into a gas bar, and Andy cut the engine. It got so quiet so abruptly, I could hear the ringing in my ears again. A thin Indigenous kid in an oversized black sweater walked out of the bar and over to the driver's side window.

"Good afternoon," the boy said.

Andy nodded hello and handed him a card and a rolled bill. The boy ambled around the back of the truck to the opposite side, and I could feel the gas lever clunk through my seat. Andy reclined in his and finally closed his eyes. I looked out the window at the boy. As he pumped, he stared out toward the road. So I looked out to the road. Then Dreadlocks turned to look out at the road, too.

"Hey," the young woman said from up front. "Next stop's not for at least an hour. So if you gotta tinkle, you'd better go now."

XV

· · · · ·

DREADLOCKS AND I waved goodbye to the green pickup truck. We were in a grocery store parking lot. The sun was setting. I had no idea which way to go next. She stretched her arms above her head, fluttered her lips, then shook out all of her limbs like she was releasing a demon.

"Come on," she said. "Let's dance."

I didn't move.

"Loosen up," she said.

I rolled my wrists, flapped my arms like a chicken. She grabbed me by the hands and shook me with force.

"Get stupid!" she yelled.

I swayed my hips a little, side to side. She let go, and I kept moving.

"Okay," I said. "Feeling stupid."

"The goal is to get stupid without feeling stupid," she said. Then pulled her rucksack, nearly the same size as her body, onto her back. "Where are you going now?"

"I'm trying to figure that out."

"Well, where are you trying to get to? Maybe I can help."

"It's far," I said. "I think. I don't really know where we are right now."

"Let me guess." She pressed her fingers into her temples. "I'm sensing there's a long lost relative of some kind. Your birth mom?"

"No."

"A twin, separated at birth?"

"I'm not looking for a long lost relative."

"No, you definitely are. I'm psychic."

"I'm going to a camp. It's a research camp. In the subarctic."

"Research for what?"

"Science. The magnetic field."

"Huh," said Dreadlocks. "I flunked out of science like three times. You must be crazy smart."

"I'm just very passionate about facts," I said.

"And you have to go all the way to the arctic to study it? What about school?"

"Subarctic."

"Right."

"Because in the subarctic is where one can find the perfect set of conditions, in terms of temperature and darkness. And coordinates, in relation to the sun. For studying. So the research camp, for school, is there."

"So, all of your equipment's in that little backpack?" she said.

"Yes. I mean, there's gear at the camp, too."

"Right." She nodded. Then tightened and buckled the straps of her bag around her body, waddled forward, and gave me a hug.

"Science is badass," she said, after letting go. "The endlessness of the universe. But then, multiple universes. Too much sugar for this human brain."

"I think it's like that for all brains," I said.

Then we said our goodbyes, and Dreadlocks set out in one of the directions, toward nothing specific, but hopefully someplace to call home for a while. My stomach coiled. I dug out the small plastic bag from my backpack, counted the twenties, the small bills, the coins. I pocketed a five and walked up to the automatic doors of the grocery store. The raw, crisp air felt cleansing. I picked up a basket and strolled each aisle, sucking on grapes I held hidden in my fist. In the cereal aisle, I opened a package of six miniature boxes, slipped three into my backpack. Opened a box of crackers and tucked a sleeve of them beneath my sweater. Then went over to the refrigerators by a closed cash. Collected a Snapple, which was the only item I placed in the basket. I thought about slipping it into my backpack, too, until I realized I was being watched by a dwarfish lady in a green apron and a hairnet pretending to weigh a cabbage with her hands. I turned my back to her and walked to an open till. She followed. Didn't take her eyes off of me until I was standing in front of the cashier.

. . .

Outside the store again, I looked for the North Star. It wasn't up yet. So I sat down on the pavement, cracked the Snapple, and waited until it was.

XVI

. . . . . .

IN SOME STORIES, Dad said, it was a date that had already passed. In others, it was far in the future, way past when everyone I knew would be dead. But for Dad it was sooner. The millennium. People across the planet were already on their way, being pulled to their place, their pole, summit, salt pan. To go to their true home. Where they would meet their true family. I told him, *You were there when we were all born. In the hospital. You saw me, and then the dogs, come out of Mom's vagina. You saw the blood and mucus and heard us breathe for the first time. You even cut those gross cord things that Mom kept wrapped in Saran wrap and taped inside our photo albums. You made us. You and Mom did.* And I remember how he looked when I said that. Like he wanted me to be right.

There was a crunch of feet, or paws, or gargoyle talons, against the dirt floor of the barn. Like someone, or something, was watching me. I paused, then continued grinding a stick against a rock. I couldn't quit thinking of Colt. His lighter. The temperature had fallen with the sun, and I was getting cold.

Another crunch, this time louder and paired with a faint whine. Whatever it was, it was creeping closer. Then two amber eyes peeked out from behind a heap of hay.

I grabbed my bag, squeezed through the heavy wooden door, and sprinted out into the field of mustard that glowed like neon beneath the moon. Until I tripped, landing upside down and backward, an arm bent up along my spine. All kinds of bright colours burst in a fireworks display behind my eyelids. Dishes crashed deep within my ears. Then just as quickly as it'd happened, everything went numb. I craned my neck to see the barn behind me. A small fox darted out, making off with my Frosted Flakes. It disappeared into a hole in the side of an old brick silo. I rolled onto my side to release my arm from beneath my body and sat up on my knees. Then immediately keeled forward and threw up from the pain.

XVII

A HORSE AND buggy clattered along the otherwise empty road. Birds chanted to the rising sun as I dragged my soles against the gravel. I wasn't sure whether or not I was supposed to stick out a thumb, so I unwound the sweater I'd wrapped around my arm like a sling and waved it like a flag.

The buggy began to slow, until the horse came to a stop.

"Little lady, you have been hurt?" said the driver. He had a German accent, a foot-long beard, suspenders, and a straw hat. Beside him sat a teenage girl in a burgundy plaid dress, a long blond braid beneath her bonnet.

"A bit," I said, re-slinging my arm.

"You have been outdoors the whole night?" he asked. "You are hobo girl?"

I sighed.

"Yes. I am. Would you be able to give me a ride?"

The horse stomped a back foot.

"Please?" I said.

The driver climbed down from his seat, walked around the side of the carriage, stood directly in front of me, and hiked up his pants. Then held out his hand.

"Give to me your package," he demanded.

I took a step back and looked up at the girl, confused. He pointed behind me.

"Your package," he said again.

"The bag," the girl said from the carriage.

"Oh," I said. "Of course. Duh."

I handed him the backpack, and he passed it up to the girl.

"Now," he said, crouching down and clasping his fingers together, "foot here."

Again, I looked to the girl.

"Put your foot in his hands," she said. "He gives you a boost."

So I put my foot in his hands. The girl reached over the side of the carriage to pull me up by my good arm. Together, they hoisted and heaved me onto the back seat.

"Is broke?" asked the girl.

"I don't know."

"You can move the fingers, no?" the man asked.

I flexed and unflexed my fingers. It felt like running my wrist through a sewing machine.

"Yes," I said.

"You can move the fingers, is good sign," the man assured me.

The girl turned in her seat. "I broke rib once," she said.

"How?"

"Horse."

"You fell from one?" I said.

"*Nein.* He did kick me. Buchweizen."

The horse pulling the buggy snorted and tossed his head.

"Him?" I said, looking at the horse.

"*Ja,*" she said. "This is Buchweizen."

The man clicked his tongue. We jerked forward.

"Hi, Buchweizen," I said.

The girl giggled.

. . .

We rolled along the straight, flat road with no end to it in sight. Somehow, though, we eventually made a turn. Then were rolling down another straight, flat, endless road. The flatness of everything dumbfounded me, like we were travelling through a dream. The sun beat down on the black hood of the carriage, and I felt a swell of nausea with each of the horse's steps. I brought my knees into my chest and closed my eyes. Drifting in and out of consciousness, I could hear Mom's whispering in the next room over. *Psycho,* and *sicko, brainwashed basket case of pure brown shit,* over and over. The twins were still potty training. There was a puddle of piss beneath the kitchen table.

Eventually, a white house came into view in the distance. The driver, Jacob, hollered to the horse as we trundled up a thin path toward it. Closer up, I could see a barn and a greenhouse tucked behind the home. The horse stopped, and the daughter, Charity, helped me out of the carriage. She guided me across the front yard, her arm linked through mine.

"What is your age? You are sixteen, I think? I am fifteen. So we are close. There are other girls this age. Kathrine, Marike. Marike is very funny."

A woman wearing the same plaid dress as Charity stepped out of the front door. She watched me closely as Jacob spoke to her in German. Then, in English, he said, "We found her by road. Her arm is hurt."

Her eyes stayed locked on me as Charity led me right in front of her face.

"I'm sorry," I said.

"For what?" the woman asked.

"I don't know," I stuttered, breaking her gaze and looking to the ground.

Charity spoke to her mother in German, too. The woman reached out to take my good hand and introduced herself as Anna, then led us inside. The house was spotless. A sofa covered in a large quilt faced a fireplace set up like a picture with three logs criss-crossed atop a light dusting of silver cinders. A cast-iron rod and a short straw broom hung beside it. Far more practical than a hole covered in twigs and wet pine needles. Anna led me to the sofa, sat me down, and untied the sweater from my arm. A large blue bruise covered the skin up to my elbow, and my wrist had swelled to twice its normal size. Anna commanded something of Charity in German, who left, then returned with ice wrapped in a handkerchief.

"Is sprain," Anna said. "Will be normal as new again in few days. You are welcome to stay for night or two. But you will need to help with the chores, as is only fair. I dictate to you the chores you can manage with injury."

She pressed the ice hard against my wrist. I let out a squeal. Then she placed my good hand on top of the kerchief and told me to hold it in place. Stood from the sofa, patted down her dress, and left the room. I looked to Charity, who was standing in front of me with an open smile across her face. I smiled back. By the window, an empty rocking chair rocked. A family photo was propped on a small table beside the couch: Jacob and Anna, Charity, and two young boys.

"Are those your brothers?" I asked.

"*Ja*. They are annoying," she laughed.

"Ha. Right. I have brothers, too."

"Really?" she asked.

"Yes," I responded.

"They are annoying, *ja*?"

She laughed again.

"They can be annoying, for sure," I said.

I removed the ice and examined my arm. My fingers looked like breakfast links.

"Where'd she go?" I asked, nodding in the direction Anna had gone.

"Back to chores. She has many to do before supper. As she is in charge of the supper."

The chair rocked again.

"Is there someone else here?" I asked.

Charity shrugged. I looked around the room.

"Guess it was just an earthquake," I said.

"You go to school?" she asked.

"No," I said. "Where do you go to school?"

"At home. Mostly I learn things now to help for chores. Like cooking, and I make clothes."

"Like, home ec?" I said.

She smiled again.

"The boys go to schoolhouse," she said.

Outside, Jacob shouted indignantly in German.

"Your brothers annoying him?" I said.

"He is unsaddling Buchweizen," Charity said.

The ice in the handkerchief was melting and dripping onto my lap. I was holding a puddle.

"Did you make the dress you're wearing?" I asked her.

"This?" She looked down and bunched up the fabric from her waist in both fists. "*Ja*. And I make Mother's. I make lots. In fact, since you supper with us, you will need one to wear, too. That" — she pointed to my crotch — "you cannot wear."

I looked down to the frayed cuffs of my shorts I'd chopped up from an old pair of jeans.

"I guess it's a lot of leg for a dinner party," I said.

She bent forward and slipped a finger beneath the strap of my tank top.

"And breast," she said.

At that moment, from nowhere, the brothers appeared, standing side by side at the other end of the couch. Sweaty with dirt stuck to their faces. Charity scolded them in German and pointed to the door, but they remained right where they were. Leering.

"I wasn't planning to stay so long," I said to Charity.

"*Nein*, is fine. Because you can borrow one of my dresses," she replied. Then she took the puddle from my hand. "Come, we will get dressed at my room now."

She hurried off down a hall from the living room, but as soon as I stood to follow, the boys scurried to block my way. One moved with a slight limp, like one leg was longer than the other, while the other boy had an oddly large brow that cast a shadow over both of his eyes. We stood, locked in a staring contest, until Charity reappeared and batted them both over the head. Then she took my good hand and pulled me away.

XVIII

THERE WAS NO disguising me in one of Charity's dresses. Even a bonnet couldn't hide the fact that I was an outsider. Men in suspenders cocked their faces at me as if I posed some kind of threat, while one at a time, I carried and set pitchers of water along the two long tables they sat at. Anna, Charity, and five other women placed steaming trays of food along a buffet.

I took my seat at the very end of a table, across from the brothers. Once all the food had been set, Charity took her seat beside me. An older man in a suit jacket and tie stood at the head of the table next to ours and led the group in a prayer. The room chorused in German. Charity recited the prayer with poise, while the brothers stared me down like some old Victorian painting. I clasped my hands together, closed my eyes, and saw the twins, lying belly-side down on the living room floor, playing tug of war with a fish stick.

After the prayer, the table next to us rose and moved in single file toward the buffet. As people returned with plates full of food, the brothers began to salivate.

"Do you eat like this every night?" I asked Charity.

"Like this?"

"A feast. All together."

Our table began to stand and line themselves up.

"Is supper."

"*Ja,*" whispered Eyebrows from across the table. "Is supper, Yulia."

"Why are you whispering?" I whispered back.

Charity nudged me and gave me a look like I'd better quit talking and start walking or else she'd sic her brothers on me. Looking over her shoulder, I realized I was holding up the line. I turned and marched forward with Charity following close behind. On the other side, the boys ran ahead. By the time we reached the buffet, most of the dishes had already been bull-dozed. The only food left untouched was a large blueberry pie. I hovered over it, closed my eyes, and inhaled deep through my nose. Then placed my hand flat on the table next to it. It was not sticky. I opened my eyes.

Once Charity had finished filling her plate and started making her way back to the table, I picked up the serving knife and cut a chunk of the pie onto my own plate. In its heap, it looked like a crushed skull. Still standing there, I took a fistful from my plate, shoved it into my mouth. Wondered if it would ever be enough.

• • •

Charity set pillows and blankets for herself on the floor.

"Please don't sleep on the floor," I said.

"For me to not offer my bed would be inhospitable," she said. Then she crossed her legs and began the delicate process of untying her very long, very tight braid. It unravelled to what appeared to be at least five feet in length.

"Have you ever had a haircut?" I said.

"Cut?"

"Your hair."

She stretched her arm, running the brush through from roots to tips.

"My hair is gift from God."

I pulled my own hair to my nose and smelled it.

"My hair stinks," I said. "It's a gift from the garbage man."

Charity gave me a vacant look.

"Pee-yew," I said, fanning my hand in front of my scrunched nose. "Gross. Yuck. Poop."

"Oh," Charity realized, "*stinken. Der gestank.*"

"Yeah, *stinken.*" I held the ponytail in her direction. "Wanna sniff?"

"Um, *nein?*" Charity said, half smiling.

"My mom used to braid my hair before I went to bed," I said. "So I'd transform into a Disney princess overnight. Really, it just transformed me into a poodle."

"Disney," Charity repeated in a tone like she was recalling her first kiss. "I have often wondered of Disney. And also, the funnies."

"Funnies? Like, comics?"

"*Nein.* Funnies with invisible laugh. Like, Lucy. Mary Tyler Moore. Seinfeld. The people are together and saying funny things. Then invisible laugh goes ha ha ha ha ha."

"That's the audience. There are people behind the cameras laughing at the jokes."

"Is lucky you get to witness such funnies. And Disney."

"I guess," I said, picturing the dogs in their skid-marked

onesies, cracking up at the dancing flubber in *Flubber* for the fiftieth time. "You must have something here, too, like TV. Or better."

"Hm," said Charity.

I scanned her very sparse room. Then looked out the window. Charity looked out the window, too.

"The sky?" she said. "Sky can be *wünderbar*. I like the moon."

I looked at the moon. It seemed closer than it'd ever been before.

"Very entertaining," I said. Then after a second, I asked her, "Do you ever see anything weird up there?"

"Why weird?"

"Strange? Not normal?"

Charity shrugged. "Yes," she said. "Now, I ask you question. For why you do leave your mutter? You have nice memories with her?"

I looked down at the bed.

"Yeah. Some nice ones."

"Is your father? Was he a beater?"

"A beater?" I laughed.

"*Ja.* Is not reason to run away? Is reason to laugh?"

"My dad didn't beat us," I said.

"You have nice memories with your father, too?"

"I have nice memories," I said, and watched as they played out like a sitcom montage against Charity's patchwork bed-spread. Dad and I at the library. Dad in front of the micro-fiche. Wearing those big squishy headphones, studying the audio tapes. Sending me on Dewey Decimal scavenger hunts. *My assistant*, he would call me, as I expertly turned thin en-cyclopedia pages, laminations of agonic and isogonic line maps through history. *You've earned your McNuggets.* But other things, too. Playing "Happy Birthday" on the harmonica for Mom. Pancakes when it rained. I didn't want to talk anymore. At least, not about the stupid sky.

"What else do you like to do for fun?" I asked Charity. "Besides watching the moon."

"Fun? I bunch with my friends? Bunch together, with my friends?"

"Like, when you're cold?"

"Sometimes we are cold. And sometimes we are warm, too. But, bunch. We do games, and sing, and speak. But not always seriously."

"Relaxed," I said.

"Yes, with laugh. And I enjoy to write." She crawled across the room and opened the bottom drawer of a dresser. Lifted out a stack of worn notebooks. "These are all of my stories. I write every day nearly, when I have completed chores."

"You're allowed to write?" I asked her.

"Allowed?"

"Like, it's okay? You have permission?"

"Why would I not have permission to write?" She tucked the books back into the drawer, then returned to her makeshift bed, where she sat up on her knees. "In the morning you do help with breakfast. You ask Anna what chores you do."

"Okay."

"How is your arm feeling? Is better?"

I lifted my arm. It felt like a wood plank with a hundred rusty nails hammered into it.

"Not really."

"Okay."

She turned off the bedside light.

"Julia?" Charity said.

"Yes?"

"You did not tell me, for why do you leave home? You are looking for gold? Or, you want to become actress in Hollywood?"

I shimmied low into the bed, pulled the bedspread up to my armpits, and gazed up at the white, cobweb-free ceiling lit by that oddly enormous moon.

"Well," I started, "I've always had this dream."

"Asleep?"

"Awake. A real-life dream. To join the circus. And like, travel all around in a circus trailer, and eat hot dogs every day."

"A circus?"

"Tightrope walkers, fire eaters. Lions. Cannons. And clowns. You'd like them, clowns. People dressed up in big wigs and funny costumes, whose only job is to make everyone laugh."

"Oh," said Charity. "I know clowns. I do like them. You would like to be a clown?"

"Yes."

I turned my head to the side to see Charity's intense, wide eyes looking back at me.

"I could not ever leave. How do I imagine life without my home?" she said.

"Well, that's a nice thing," I said.

"But I do believe the circus would be magic place to be," she said. "And I do think you will make great clown."

"Thanks," I said.

"Now, I am going to pray. You can pray also, if you like."

She closed her eyes, tilted her forehead toward the floor, and spoke quietly in German for several minutes. I clasped my hands together, too, and prayed. To the god of the ants for more blueberry pie.

XIX

· · · · · ·

ANNA ASSIGNED ME egg duty, for which Charity gave me a yellow dress to wear. Trekking out into the pink morning, I had to hold the dress up to keep from tripping on it while carrying the basket Anna had hooked to my elbow beneath a sling she'd fashioned out of a dishtowel. Charity'd practically glided off in the opposite direction, toward the stable.

Inside the barn were rows upon rows of nesting boxes surrounding an open space of hay where the hens could roam. I plucked an egg from the ground and placed it into a basket. Then another, and another. I was feeling proud of myself, doing such a good job collecting eggs. Until the fourth, which I fumbled. It dropped from my hand and fractured, spilling orange goo onto the hay. I tried to cover it with more hay, until a giggle echoed up along the roof of the barn. I paused.

"Hey," I called out.

No movement, no response. As if I'd imagined it. I looked down at the hay. Kicked it again. Then more giggling. Two small silhouettes hovered near the far end of the barn.

"What are you doing?" I shouted.

"Pink sky at night is sailor's delight," one sang out.

"But pink sky in morning is sailor's warning," recited the other.

"Kay," I called back. "Don't you have a schoolhouse to get to?"

"Julia."

I jumped. Charity was suddenly standing right behind me.

"Charity," I said, "can you and your brothers please stop appearing out of nowhere?"

"Hi, Julia," she said again.

"Hi, Charity."

"You have seen Paul and Peter?" she asked.

"Eyebrows and Gimpy?"

I turned to face the other end of the barn. They were no longer anywhere to be seen.

"They were here a second ago," I said.

"Is scoliosis, Julia. You do know where they have gone?"

"I swear, they were just here." I pointed with my good hand. "Over there."

Charity did a half twirl and again, floated her way out of the barn. My arm was getting tired; the three eggs in the basket were starting to feel like three dozen. I looked down at the mess of yolk and hay like a kindergarten craft. What was I doing on this farm? In this dress? I threw the whole basket onto the ground, then. I wanted the mess to be worse. I stomped on the eggs, kicked up the hay. Then found more eggs, and destroyed them, too. Like I couldn't stop. Until my foot landed on something plump and soft. But also kind of hard. And definitely gross.

. . .

"Jacob, there's something you should see."

Jacob dumped a bucket of pumpkin sludge into the pig slough.

"What is, Julia?"

"I think it's a dead chicken. But I could be wrong."

He placed the bucket down on the ground.

"A dead chicken is dead chicken, Julia," he said.

"Well, whatever it is, it's over there by the eggs. I just thought you should know."

Jacob hiked up his pants and told me to lead the way, then remained a consistent two steps behind me. As we walked, I tried to figure out what I would tell him. That I'd dropped the eggs by accident. And stepped on them by accident, too.

"See," I said, once we were inside the barn. I pointed down at the lump. "It's kind of buried still."

He motioned for me to step aside. Then bent down and brushed away the yolky hay, uncovering the fowl's carcass. Beheaded. He took a deep breath then.

"Is hen, Julia."

"I dropped the eggs," I said. "By accident. And I stepped on them by accident, too."

He removed his hat, wiped the sweat from his brow with his forearm.

"Is okay, Julia. You go find Anna now."

"Is that normal?" I asked. "Does that happen on farms?"

He shrugged. Put his hat back on.

"Is peculiar."

I nodded, unable to turn from the massacre.

"In kitchen is where is Anna. You help her now."

"Okay," I said. "Sorry."

"What sorry for now?"

"The eggs. It was an accident."

He turned his back to me then, casting his great bearded shadow over the dead creature.

. . . .

Walking toward the house, I could hear the sound of a hammer hammering on metal someplace off in the distance. Over and over in the otherwise silent day. I opened the door into the empty living room and, for a moment, held my breath, listening. Still, nothing but the distant hammer. I crept down the hall as quietly as possible toward Charity's bedroom, ready to ditch the dress, collect my backpack, and go before anyone could notice. But as I pushed open the bedroom door, I nearly screamed.

"What doing, Yulia?"

The boys stood side by side in their dirty garden boots on top of Charity's pillow bed. My bag was in Scolio's hand, unzipped, its contents dumped across the floor.

"Jesus Christ," I said.

"Jesus, Christ?" Eyebrows asked.

"What the heck are you doing?" I said.

"What are you doing?" he responded.

"You killed hen, Yulia!" Scoliosis exclaimed. "We must search for head. You hide head in here."

"What? No I didn't."

Anna called their names from the kitchen.

"Yes," he continued. "You breaking eggs in barn. You have devil spirit."

I grabbed my bag.

"Don't touch my stuff," I said, and began picking up my belongings.

"Watch out, Yulia," said Scolio, drawing out the *u* until I felt it crawling down my neck. "There are always eyes seeing."

"And ears always hearing words," said Eyebrows.

They stepped off the pillow bed and walked past me out the door. I slammed it behind them and, one-handed, tore off the dress. Pulled on my normal clothes, inside out, picked up my bag, and went to make my escape. Down the hall, through the living room. But of course, Anna was already standing at the door, tall and obstructive, wiping her hands against her apron.

"Julia?" she asked. "Where are eggs?"

• • •

Again, the boys stared me down from across the supper table. I nudged Charity, but the second she looked up, they looked away, and all I received was a stern frown that made her look like a young Anna in training as she continued to recite the prayer.

• • •

Mom dropped four pieces of white bread into the toaster and pressed the lever. It sprang back. She unplugged it, then plugged it back in. Still it sprang back. She pressed the lever with two fingers, then the side of her hand, as though she were karate-chopping the thing into working. Then she just held it down, hard, with the type of pressure that turned her fingers white, pink at the tips. Face turning the same colours. The twins, flinging spoonfuls of milk and Fruity O's at the walls, paused. Asked her what the matter was. Where was their toast. Why weren't they eating their toast yet. She let go. Then ripped the toaster from the wall, pushed it off the counter.

"Everything is something!" she yelled.

The O's that had stuck slid slowly toward the floor like slugs, leaving streaks of purple, blue, yellow goo.

"Where's toast?" said the twins.

KATHRINE WORE A bonnet and a black-and-white plaid dress. Marike wore a bonnet and a blue-and-white plaid dress. Charity wore a bonnet and a red-and-white plaid dress with a yellow rose sewn into the collar, while I wore a bonnet and a new, clean, green-and-white plaid dress. We all leaned against a fence, looking outward, like characters in a book. Marike spun a stem of barley between her palms.

"Kathrine's sister is to be married soon," Charity told me.

"And I am most excited," said Marike.

"Why are you excited for?" said Kathrine.

"The party," said Marike. "I love the wedding party."

"Kathrine is artist. She is very good in draw-er," said Charity.

"In?" I repeated.

"In painting and also in draw," said Marike. "Like pictures. She can draw faces of family."

I nodded.

"I'd love to see sometime," I said to Kathrine.

"You can," Charity said. "In our home. In mother's cupboard is invitation and is draw by Kathrine. And painted. Is *wunderschön.*"

"*Aufhören*, Charity," Kathrine cut in. "I do not want to continue talk of this anymore."

"She is blush," Marike teased, whisking the head of the barley against Kathrine's cheek. Kathrine slapped it away.

"*Nein!*" she snapped.

Marike and Charity froze. I froze, too. Then slowly, we settled back against the fence.

"Her sister leaves," Charity said. "Goes to different colony."

Kathrine stared across the field without looking at the field.

"Where you come from, you have funny, right? You have Jim Carrey. And you have Carrot Top?" Marike asked me.

"Yes. But Carrot Top isn't really funny," I said. "How do you know about them?"

"Magazines. Is hidden. But you know, I like to make people laugh. Where you come from, everyone is always laughing."

"People laugh here, too, right?" I said. "Charity told me."

"Yes, but not like you people." Marike smiled. "You people always laughing at sex."

"Marike!" Charity slapped her shoulder. "Listen to your mouth."

"It's just a word," I said.

"Is not good. Is lousy," said Charity.

Marike giggled.

"Is wrong," Charity said, looking back and forth at both of us, her face clenching.

"*Ja*, is dirty," Marike said, then tickled Charity's cheek with the barley. "Sex sex sexy!" she sang. Then she turned to Kathrine — "Lillian will be making sexy after the wedding!" — and tickled her, as well. Charity snatched at the grain and snapped the stem, then tossed it as hard as she could. It landed a foot in front of her. Marike sighed. We resumed our positions.

"How long do you stay here for?" Kathrine asked.

"She stays until her arm is healed," said Charity.

"How is it you hurt it?" asked Marike.

"It's stupid," I said.

"Ha, stupid," Marike repeated. Then deepened her voice, "I like the word, *stupid*."

"No," said Charity.

"Well, it was stupid," I said. "I tripped and fell in a mustard field."

All three bonnets tilted toward me. A bird warbled from farther down the fence.

"I was being chased by a fox. Or it could've been something else. Like a wolf. I don't know. It was dark."

"*Meine Güte*," Marike whispered.

"Fox will not hunt for person. We have many fox here. Catch mice, eat crops. But will not hunt for people," Charity said. Then she smiled. "You scared for not good reason."

"Yes. Fox pest, but runs away when it sees person," said Kathrine.

"So, maybe was wolf!" said Marike, grabbing my unslung hand and jumping. "Or maybe, was witch!"

"Probably a witch," I said.

"Or man," she continued, louder, "looking for sex sex sexy!"

"Halt, Marike," Charity said in her Anna voice.

Marike rolled her eyes.

"Where is it you leave to once healed?" Kathrine asked.

A cowbell rang in the distance.

"She will go to find her dream," Charity said. "It is in the circus."

"Leave? She cannot leave!" said Marike. "We need her. She knows all of the bad words, I know it."

"We must go now," Charity said to me, taking my hand from Marike.

"What for?" I said.

"Is Mutter ringing bell. We go do wash now. Come."

. . .

As we walked back to the house, I asked Charity if she thought a fox could have gotten into the barn and eaten that chicken's head.

"Is hen," she said.

She walked fast. I had to jog to keep up.

"I forgot, before," I said, "that it's like, a whole different world here."

"Is no different world. Is same world you and everybody else like you live on," Charity said. "Maybe if there are less of dirty jokes and Jim Carreys and carrot men, this world would be happier place, and we would all of us live more in peace."

"I think the point of Jim Carrey is to make the world a happier place," I said. But she didn't respond. I fell back again as we walked a narrow path through some tall grass toward the back of the house. Anna was already standing at the door, two wooden baskets of laundry stacked beside her. Charity stopped, turned to face me, and gently placed a hand on my shoulder.

"Is okay, Julia. Is good to be funny. And is good to be person who goes to look for dream. But bad words are bad for spirit and so, bad for journey, also."

I nodded.

"I get it," I said.

She lowered her hand, then lifted the hem of her skirt and sailed toward Anna, who was holding out the yellow dress I'd worn to collect the eggs, then tried to leave behind during my great escape. Once we were close enough to see it, she extended the sleeve. It was smeared with blood.

"This will need soak," she said, handing it to Charity while keeping her eyes on me.

Charity frowned.

"*Ich kann es selbst machen*," she said to Anna. "She needs to rest arm."

"I can help," I said.

"*Nein*," said Charity, lifting both baskets with a grunt. "Is fine."

She carried the baskets around the back of the house. I looked up at Anna, whose pursed lips could have sliced a bird's neck.

"I don't know where it came from," I said. "I swear."

She went inside, and I continued to stand there, staring at the door, not sure if I was supposed to follow her inside until she barked at me to do so. Then she handed me a scrubbing brush.

"One hand can clean kitchen floor," she said.

XXI

CHARITY SAT CROSS-LEGGED on her pillow bed.

"I didn't do that to the chicken," I said.

"Mm."

She continued to write in her notebook.

"You believe me, right?" I said.

"What are you meaning?"

"I'm meaning, you know I didn't do it."

"Do what?"

"Kill that chicken."

"Is hen, Julia."

"Hen. Whatever."

"The hen brings us eggs, Julia."

"Oh my God, Charity. You don't have to tell me that hens bring eggs. The point is, you know I didn't do it, right?"

"God?"

I lay down in the bed, my back to her, pretending to sleep. Plugged my ears against the scratching pen. Eventually, she closed her book and turned off the light. Minutes later, she was lightly snoring. I rolled onto my back and looked up at the ceiling. Despite the lack of streetlights or nearby houses, the room was bright; that moon was like a spotlight from outer space.

Charity's snoring, which she'd clearly inherited from Jacob, who could be heard from across the hall and through both doors, grew deeper, and I climbed out of the bed. Collected my bag and pulled it on over the Jan Brady nightgown Charity had given me to wear. Turned the doorknob slowly with my fingertips, as if that would make less noise. I looked back at Charity, her ten-feet-long yellow hair splayed across the bedroom floor like a field of wheat. A Disney princess. The wheat one. Then I left. Hurried down the hallway to the front of the house, slipped on my shoes, and slid back the gold chain that locked the door.

"Where do you leave to this time of night?"

I jumped. The twins stood side by side in front of the fireplace, their pale faces like two grey orbs floating in the dark room.

"What are you doing?" I whispered. "Why aren't you two in bed?"

"Is dangerous at night," said Eyebrows. "For coyotes and bears."

"I'm aware," I said.

"As well," Scolio added, "the night is when dark spirits wander the Earth."

"Thanks," I said. "I'll be careful."

They tittered in tandem, until Scolio let loose a large yawn. His brother elbowed him in the ribs.

"Sleepy, gremlins?" I said. "Past your bedtime?"

I turned and opened the door. Eyebrows shouted after me.

"You will be going to hell, Yulia!"

I turned back to him, pressing my finger to my lips. He held out his open palm, upon which lay a small dark lump.

"What is that?" I whispered. "Did you poo in your hand?"

He stepped closer, displaying a dead mouse with its feet chopped off. I let out a small yelp, then covered my mouth.

"You murdered him?" I screeched through my fingers.

"*Nein*," he replied. "Is was our friend. His was name Klaus. It was you who did hurt Klaus. Just like you hurt hen."

"I didn't kill that hen!" I whispered.

"You lie, Yulia. You lie about the hen, you lie about the circus. You lie about map, and Egg Island. You lie about everything."

He pitched the dead critter at me. I squeezed my eyes shut, flapping both my good and not good arm in front of my face. Then the lights turned up, and I opened my eyes. Jacob stood beside the oil lamp on the mantle. The twins had entirely vanished.

"Julia?" he said. "What is it you are doing at door?"

I looked down at the tiny, dismembered carcass crumpled at my feet.

"*Was ist im Namen Gottes geschehen?*" he gasped.

XXII

THE BUGGY WHEELS caused a racket in the dead of night. Buchweizen's head bobbed up and down with each step, while mine twisted in circles around itself. Had I blacked out like some sick killer and chopped off that poor hen's head? Or were those two little deformed poltergeists trying to sabotage me? Was I dreaming? Was I schizophrenic?

We stopped outside a truck-stop diner. Four semitrailers were parked in the lot.

"I do not wish to see you in danger, Julia," Jacob said, his voice deep and even.

"Then why are you leaving me in the middle of nowhere with a bunch of lonely truck drivers?" I blurted in response.

"Inside, you do ask for Miss Maggie. She will offer safe place for sleep tonight."

"How far are we from civilization?"

"You just come from civilization."

"The other kind."

Jacob cleared his throat.

"In car, perhaps less than one hour to nearest town."

I punched the bruise on my wrist, then cried out in pain.

"What do such thing for?" Jacob said.

"I could never kill something, Jacob. Seriously."

His gaze fell to the reins resting in his grip. I climbed down from the buggy. Then stood there and frowned back up at him.

"So, bye, I guess," I said.

"May Lord take mercy on you, Julia. I wish not for you to find more pain or death on your journey."

I turned away from him then and walked toward the light of the diner.

"Yeah," I shouted back. "Same."

· · ·

The diner hummed with the drone of an old ventilation system that was partially visible along the roof as if it were part of the decor. I took a seat on a stool at the counter and watched the television sitting on top of a refrigerator. A plane crashed silently into the Pacific ocean. By the window, a table of three burly men looked down into their white cylindrical mugs that looked like toy teacups in their giant hands. Two tables in front of them, a much skinnier man with thick glasses and suspenders glanced at me quickly, then looked back down at the red basket of chicken nuggets in front of him. Ashed a cigarette onto a small plate of ketchup. I traced over a circular water stain on the counter in front of me. No radio, no music.

Miss Maggie backed out through a swinging door. She wore a stained floral apron over her jeans and a soft purple turtleneck. Her hair, dark and streaked with thick white strands, was rolled up and folded into a clip at the base of her head like a ball of yarn. She looked at me, confused.

"Hello, little girl," she said with a German accent.

"Hi," I replied. "Do you know Jacob with the horse and buggy?"

"Yes?"

"He told me to ask for Miss Maggie."

"Okay," she said. "Would you like tea?"

"Yes," I said. "I would very much like tea. Thank you."

She prepared a red mug the size of a bowl, then placed it directly beneath my chin. I inhaled the steam. It warmed my face, cheeks, and nose. Felt like it was hugging my brain.

"Why Jacob does bring you this time of night? Wait," she held up a hand to stop herself. "Tea first, questions two. My apologies."

"He mentioned I might be able to stay with you," I said.

"My apartment is upstairs."

There was a shuffle behind us as the four men pushed back their chairs and prepared to leave, sucking the last sips from their mugs. As they made their way out the door, each nodded in our direction and said, "Thanks again, Miss Maggie." She waved back and replied, "I see you soon, boys." The bell dinged as they pushed through the door. Miss Maggie smiled at me.

"So, little girl. Is job you looking for? Because I can make job."

"I just need a place to sleep. I'll be out of your way once the sun comes up."

"You are alone?"

I nodded. She frowned.

"Your family is near?"

I shook my head no.

"Okay."

She walked out from behind the counter to clean up the table the men had just left. Pocketed the change left behind into her apron. When she returned, she looked me over for a moment, hands on her hips.

"You drink tea now," she said. "So we can speak better."

I held the hot mug to my lips and sipped.

"Jacob is brother of mine," she said.

"Really?"

I imagined her slender cheeks covered in a knotty beard.

"*Ja*. I grew up in community. I leave at twenty years of age. I suffered long of conflicting morals. I was devout, and yet I could not be happy, as I could not marry man happy. I desired for a woman."

"Were you kicked out?"

"Is was my choice to go. My brother begged me to stay. However, I realized I could not live in place where I could not be outside who I was inside. So I left."

"And went, down the road?"

"Down the road? No. I travelled far. I travelled first to United States, California. The desert. And then to Rocky Mountains, Colorado. I even visited to Las Vegas, Nevada, the land of sin."

She winked.

"Then I wanted to go farther, so I took plane to Germany, and visit Austria, and the land where we come from. And I remember standing in rolling green field and looking out at the Alps mountains and feeling so very, very small, and so very, very alone. But so very, very at peace. *God is not over top these mountains*, I thought to myself. *God is the feeling I have when I look at these mountains*. And then I felt, for certain, whatever I need in journey of life, I can find inside of myself."

I looked down into the liquid at the bottom of my mug. Pictured a young Miss Maggie standing in the foothills of the Alps. Apron-free and surrendered.

"You, little girl, must be exhausted. Please do follow me."

I stood from the stool and pulled my backpack over one shoulder. Realized I hadn't even noticed the skinny man leave. Hadn't heard the bell above the door, or seen the lights from his truck flood the window. Miss Maggie gestured for me to bring along my tea. I followed her past a washroom and up a small flight of stairs. Then through a door, which opened into a small room with a bed, sink, and rug. Framed landscapes of prairie storms hung on the walls. Ceramic horses were propped on a bookshelf amongst cookbooks and ancient-looking atlases.

"You are okay to sleep on cot?"

She slid a rollaway bed out from a closet behind the door.

"Cot's perfect," I said.

"Now, you can tell me," she said. "How you did end up with Jacob in community?"

"He found me. I was trying to catch a ride."

Miss Maggie nodded.

"And so, why does he bring you here now?"

"I think he thinks I'm a witch."

"Ah," she said. "So, is toilet behind that curtain. My apologies for lack of door. But we are all both of us ladies here, anyway. Now, I will find you blankets for cot because, as you can see, it is little cold."

She hauled a pink comforter from the top shelf of the closet.

"Do you get company often?" I asked.

"No. However, I do have niece, and I like for her to know she has place to come."

She spread the blanket over the cot, then stood tall, proudly surveying the made-up bed.

"All right. Is ready for dreaming," she said.

I thanked her and sat down on the cot. Still holding the warm cup in my lap.

"Okay, little girl. I go back downstairs now. Soon I will return. Please do be at home."

She closed the door, and I listened to her steps, down the stairs below me. Then gone. Repeated to myself: as you can see, it is little cold.

XXIII

I WOKE UP to three fried eggs, six triangles of buttered toast, and a mass of hash browns.

"For before your journey," she said.

She placed the serving tray holding the plate on the floor beside the cot. I sat up and examined the bruise on my arm. It was now yellow and green and shaped like Australia. A ray of sunlight through the small round window cut through the centre of the room, illuminating dust particles. Miss Maggie filled a kettle at the sink. Her hair was undone and reached to her waist. It was almost as long as Charity's.

"You do need plate of ketchup?" she asked me.

"Sure," I replied.

She put the kettle on the stove and pulled a glass ketchup bottle from the fridge. Set it beside my tray along with a second small plate.

"You tell me where you are going to?" she asked me.

I wrenched open the ketchup bottle. Tipped it upside down and shook. Nothing came out. Beat the end with my open palm.

"Honestly," I said, "I think I'll just know when I'm there."

The ketchup dropped out in a ball. I set the bottle on the floor, then picked up a piece of toast.

"Or, I won't," I said. "You don't like haircuts either?"

"I cut hair one time. After leaving community. I met a girl and she cut my hair short like boy in bathroom of gas station. In Casper, Wyoming. It was for fun. But I cried and cried."

"Because of the gift from God thing?"

"Ha," said Miss Maggie. "Because I looked like ugly boy."

. . .

That morning, I stepped out into the middle of nowhere. A humid haze hung over the horizon. Yet again, I was slogging through a ditch beside a highway, kicking garbage beneath my feet: single shoes, dirty diapers. A plastic Coke bottle filled with piss, chucked from a car window. My arm was snug in the dishtowel I'd stolen from Anna, backpack tight over my shoulders. Maybe I was a serial farm-animal killer. Or a little girl, lost and far from home. Or dead right then, for all I knew. Just another highway ghost looking to cause some mysterious, tragic accident. It didn't matter. What mattered was getting to where I needed to go. Which seemed to be changing with each new road I ended up on.

XXIV

· · · · · · · ·

SOON I WAS curled between manure sacks and stacks of hay in the bed of a pickup truck, sitting across from a man who didn't know his own name. His face looked like a chunk of meteorite. He asked if he could draw my portrait, and I didn't say yes or no, just asked him what was in the little potato sack he kept tucked by his feet. He picked it up, gave it a shake. It sounded like a bag of rocks. He untied its string, and from within, pulled a shred of yellow paper and chunk of coal. Then proceeded to draw. While he worked, he told me of a place I could go. He said it had been his home once. He would tell the driver when to stop. That stop didn't come for a long, long time, it seemed. I kept myself awake by humming a made-up tune. Somehow, though, the man was able to hum along with me perfectly.

XXV

I LOOKED UP at the turrets of a Victorian mansion. Flags from different countries hung in all the windows. Upon the veranda that wrapped around the house sat a young man with a braided beard and a *WAR IS OVER* T-shirt. He rocked back and forth on a chair swing while strumming an out-of-tune guitar. As I approached the steps, he paused. Then strummed a wonky chord and bowed his head in my direction.

"Namaste," he said.

"Hi," I said.

"Bum a smoke?"

"Sorry," I replied.

The wood was flaked with chipped white paint. A small piece of square notepaper taped above the doorknob read, *push, don't turn!!!!* with a peace sign drawn in yellow highlighter below. So I pushed and entered a dim foyer that smelled like socks and burnt flowers. Delicate bells chimed from above.

Inside, a young man who looked pretty much the same as the guitar player on the veranda sat behind a small desk. His curly hair reached his shoulders, bare beneath a grey tank top with a large wolf on the front.

"*Kia ora*," he said.

"Yes," I replied.

"Welcome home."

"Right. Thanks."

I looked around the room. A tall rotary-style telephone like some artifact in a museum was propped on a phone book on top of a wooden bench in one corner. A family of hand-painted wood ducks in the other. Black-and-white photographs hung crooked on the walls: a decomposing fox being eaten by a crow; a cut tree stump's life lines; an extreme close-up of an elderly Indigenous woman's face, the reflection of a gun in her pupil.

"Let's get you settled in, then," he said. "What's your name?"

I shrugged the bag off my shoulder, dropped it to the floor, and dug to the bottom. Pulled out the money bag and scooped two handfuls of change onto the counter.

"Julia," I said.

He handed me a key attached to a miniature troll doll.

"Down that hall, take the stairs on the left. Girls' bedroom's got the hen on the door. Shower's at the end of the hall. If you need anything, my name's Ocean."

"Thanks, Ocean," I said.

I tucked the troll key into my towel sling and started in the direction he'd pointed.

"I'm so happy you're here, Julia," he called after me. I looked back at him.

"Okay, Ocean," I said again.

· · ·

I wandered through what felt like several eternal hallways, searching for the stairs, until I found myself in a room where a group of people were playing cards around a coffee table, betting nuts, raisins, cigarettes. Above them, a giant chandelier hung in the centre of the ceiling. Thick strings of silver dust dangled amongst the crystals. Bookshelves stuffed with paperbacks, guidebooks, and board games were stacked against a wall. It smelled like everything had been there forever. Including the people.

At the other side of the room was a door. I walked over, pushed it open and found myself outside again. A girl with a dark tan and long sandy hair perched on a stool in front of an easel, painting. Beneath the easel, an orange cat missing a piece of one ear batted at a dandelion.

"Excuse me," I said.

She looked up and smiled. I held out my troll key.

"I'm lost," I said.

She stuck her paintbrush between her teeth. Took the key, examined it, then handed it back to me, leaving a smudge of green across the troll's belly.

"Back through that room. Down the hall. Turn right. There's a door. The door's got a bison painted on it. That takes you to the western stairwell."

"Bison," I said. "Got it."

I turned to go back inside, then stopped.

"What are you painting?" I asked the girl.

She invited me closer. I stepped behind and looked over her shoulder at the canvas. It looked like a woman breastfeeding a gargoyle.

"It's an abstract," she said.

"I see it," I said.

"See what?"

I pointed my slung elbow at the door. "Do all of these people live here?"

She shrugged.

"Where did you come from?" she asked me.

I pointed at the fence.

"Elma? Nutmik Lake?" she said.

"Yes," I said.

"You were working at the alpaca farm?"

"Yes," I said again. "I was doing that."

"You met Merlin?"

"I did, yes. Anyway, thanks for the directions."

I turned to leave again.

"Did an alpaca do that?"

I turned back around. She nodded at my arm.

"Just an accident," I said. "Minor alpaca feeding accident."

"Does it hurt?"

"No. A little."

She stood from the stool.

"What's your name?" she asked me.

"Julia."

She bent in front of me and marked the towel with a small greenish-brownish *J*.

"So glad you made it, Julia. My name is Sunshine."

. . .

The bedroom walls were painted with purple and yellow flowers that grew up from the floors and crept all around the furniture. Two bunks were pushed against either wall with a window between them. I dropped my bag down on a bottom bed and climbed in after it. Removed the sling from my arm, lay on my back, and closed my eyes, listening to the birds and some kind of drum somewhere outside.

Until a whimpering from above broke through the rhythm. The drumming intensified, faster and faster, before stopping abruptly. Then, sniffles. I shifted to the edge of the mattress and looked up. Above, straight black hair stuck to a small, wet face. Glassy blue eyes fixed on me, not blinking.

"I didn't know someone else was here," I said.

She squeaked like a cat toy.

"Are you okay?" I asked her.

She flipped over, hiding her face.

"Are you sick? Do you need medicine?"

"Cramp," she said into her pillow.

"A cramp?"

She rolled onto her back.

"Cramp. Pain. I have been awake so many, many hours," she continued. "The birds do not stop their singing. They cause me to feel mental."

I looked to the window. The pane was propped open by a small piece of wood. I stood from the bed, walked over to the window, and closed it, shutting out the noise. Then pulled the curtains together.

"Better?" I asked.

She didn't respond. Just sniffled more.

"Need anything else?" I said.

"Umma," she said. "My mom."

"Does she live here, too?" I said.

"No."

"Can you call her?"

She began to sob again.

"It is five o'clock in the morning there," she said.

I reached up and brushed the hair off her face. After a moment, she calmed.

"You miss your mom, too?" she asked.

I lowered my hand.

"Maybe just close your eyes," I said.

. . . .

The shower sprinkled like light rain with the occasional burst of pressure, as though some heavy cloud were passing overhead. Hair and unspecified fuzzes stuck to the stall walls and floor. Which did kind of make it feel like home. I worked a cracked bar of green soap into a lather and scrubbed at the skin around my ankle for several moments before realizing it wasn't dirt, just a sock line. My shins and knees were sore to touch, as if they were bruised all the way through to the marrow. The tan on my legs was cut bluntly mid-thigh where my shorts stopped, while the arm that had been swathed for days was two shades lighter than the other. I had turned into the innards of an old avocado.

Once finished, I reached around the curtain to find my towel was no longer on the hook where I'd hung it. I stuck my head out of the shower. Propped on the radiator, just out of reach, it had somehow folded itself into a swan.

XXVI

I SWUNG ON the chair swing upon the veranda. Along the horizon, a black dot skipped like a stone over water. I blinked.

"Hey."

I placed a foot down on the wood. Stopped the chair.

"Look what the chicken dragged in."

There, behind me, leaned against the door with his arms crossed over his chest, was Colt. Looking me up and down, half smirking, shaking his head like he'd been expecting this all along. I opened my mouth, but nothing came out. He unfolded his arms. Waved hello.

"It's me," he said. "Colt."

I stabbed my thigh with a fingernail. I was alive.

"From last week," he said.

"I know who you are," I yelled.

"Why are you shouting?" he said.

"What the heck are you doing here?"

"I came over to say hi," he said.

He walked out from the doorway and took a seat at the other end of the swing. Stretched out his long legs and began rocking the chair rigorously, back and forth. Then pulled his lighter from his pocket and flicked it. My flannel was tied around his waist. After a few flicks, he set the flame to torch.

"How'd you get my shirt?" I said.

"From off your bunk."

"You just went in there and helped yourself?"

"You weren't using it."

"Colt, what are you doing here? Like here here?" I said.

"More like, what are you doing here?" he said. "And why the heck did you abandon me? And why the heck heck are you carrying a dirty towel around like that?"

XXVII

COLT LIVED AT the top of the house. The ceiling above his bunk slanted into a peak ten feet above our heads. He pushed me up the ladder and onto his bed, his hand on my back to keep me balanced as I climbed with one arm.

"Why do I have to go up here?"

"It's my place," he said.

On the bed I tucked my legs beneath myself. Colt climbed up after me, then hooked his feet to the guardrails and fell over the side. The bunk lifted slightly and dropped as he hung upside down like a kid on monkey bars. I grabbed hold of the railing. He flipped himself back up. Hair whipped backward. Nostrils flared.

"I always wanted a bunk bed," he said. "But there was only ever one of me."

For a moment I imagined two Colts stacked in their beds, legs sticking three feet out from the ends.

"How did you find this place?" I asked him.

"I drove. Until I ran out of gas, and these hippies helped me push my car."

"Why didn't they push you to a gas station?"

"I didn't have any money for gas."

"How have you been paying for this bunk bed?"

"I contribute, and they let me stay for free. That's how it works."

He hooked his feet and hung upside down again.

"I thought you would have gone back home," I said.

He swung himself back up.

"I was going to. 'Cause I was so mad at you for ditching me. But it was raining so hard, I figured I should go and find you first."

Clothing was scattered all over the room. A towel swan was set on the bottom bunk across from us.

"So," he continued, "I drove until it was really dark out, but I didn't find you. I didn't know how you could have disappeared so quickly, the way you did. Except, obviously, the obvious."

"Obvious what?" I said.

He pointed up at the ceiling, to a yellow water stain shaped like the sun.

"Aliens. So I pulled over to think about it and slept in the car for the night. In the back seat, where you slept. Way better than sleeping in the front seat. I could actually stretch my legs out without bumping them off the steering wheel. Then it rained off and on all night. In the morning when it was all done, I started driving again, through many puddles, and realized I'd been going a little backward. There'd been an eagle's nest on the right side of the road the day before, and then I passed it again, but now it was on the left. So I drove into a city to find directions and parked by this lookout. There was this big mountain in the water called the Sleeping Giant. I know, because I got this information thing from an information booth. What are we talking about again?"

"You?" I said.

"Anyway." He reached under the mattress and pulled out a folded brochure. "See? It looks like a giant lying down."

I looked at the picture.

"Get it?"

I squinted.

"Can't you see it?" he said.

"I don't know."

"Are your eyes okay?"

"I can see it," I said.

"It's what you can call a phenomenon, Julia. It's more than just seeing. The legend says that it was a giant who turned to stone to protect a silver mine from white men. The giant's name is Nanabijou. It's an Ojibwa legend. It's all right here."

He handed me the brochure.

"After that, I got some McDonald's fries and talked to Matt, the information booth guy. He told me he was studying in university to be a scientist. Of the environment. I told him I might go to college one day. Once I figure out what I'm good at. And he was like, 'Hey man, everyone's good at something.' And I said, 'I don't know what my something is yet.' My grandma was good at baking, so she became a baker. And my grandpa was good at gas, so he became a gas station owner. Some people just know. And other people have to wait for the answer, sometimes for a long time. Then I asked him if he wanted a fry, and he told me some stuff about moss and trees, and a couple other things to go see before I left. Some historical monuments and trains. And he offered me some weed for the road. I said no. You can't drive on weed. But I did go and see those historical monuments and trains. Then I started driving again. In the right direction this time. Or at least, the direction that led me to here. On the way I stopped at a huge hole in the ground with a waterfall and a river at the bottom. It looked like a crater. Like a comet hit it. Probably one did back in dino time. Then I stopped at a diner called Maggie's. The creepy old woman named Maggie who worked there, she gave me some tea, and I slept in the parking lot. And the next morning, I ended up here. But not right here."

He pointed to the wall on the other side of the room.

"Over there a little."

He stopped talking then. I placed the brochure on the mattress between us.

"Wow," I said.

He nodded. "I won't lie. It got lonely."

I looked back at the swan.

"What about you?" he asked me.

"I walked," I said.

He jumped to the floor. Then reached his arm deep under the mattress, searching, and pulled out something small. Hid it behind his back.

"That reminds me. That I almost forgot. I got a present for you," he said. "In case I ever saw you again.

He stood a small figurine of Terry Fox atop the brochure, its plastic face somewhat smushed on one side. As though someone had tried to melt it with a lighter. It appeared cycloptic. I looked at Colt.

"It reminded me of you," he said.

XXVIII

COLT LED THE way through a maze of halls and doors and stairwells covered in washed-out, flowery wallpapers.

"Have you ever siphoned gas before?" he asked.

"Have you?" I replied.

"No. But there's gotta be someone around here who has."

We passed a room lit only by candles. Inside, four girls were seated around a Ouija board.

"Hurry," Colt said over his shoulder.

"Why? We aren't going anywhere," I said.

"I can't devise plans on an empty stomach."

At the end of one hall, we opened a door that led to a stairwell spiralling downward.

"Where do we get food?" I asked Colt.

"People leave stuff around. Spaghetti, bread. Condiments. I have a secret stash."

At the bottom of the staircase, we went through another door and found ourselves in a large kitchen. At its centre was a wooden table where people stood chopping and dicing and shredding. Others bustled around them, orbiting one another, carrying steaming pots and plates. It looked like a restaurant in Santa's workshop. I noticed Sunshine leaned against a wall, spinning a braid into her hair. Standing next to her, stirring a large pot, was Dreadlocks.

"Rotini, spaghettini, or linguine?" Colt said.

"No," I whispered.

"Speak up," he said.

Dreadlocks turned from the stove and dumped whatever food she was cooking onto two plates. Set the pot down and wiped her nose ring with the back of her hand. Sunshine handed her a fork. I turned my back to them and looked for Colt, who'd disappeared. So I looked for the door from which we had just emerged. It, too, had seemingly vanished.

"There's no red sauce," Colt said, suddenly reappearing in front of me. "But I found some honey mustard."

"We have to go."

I took two steps forward. He placed his hand on my shoulder to stop me.

"It's not that bad," he said.

"I'm not hungry," I said.

"Julia, it's honey. Honey mustard," he said.

"Hey, you."

I turned around. Dreadlocks was standing behind me.

"The professor," she said. "Shouldn't you be in the arctic by now?"

Sunshine stood beside her, holding a plate of macaroni and hot dogs. She still had paint beneath her nails.

"What happened to your arm?" asked Dreadlocks.

A metal pan fell to the floor. We all looked in the direction of the noise. Then the three of them all looked back at me.

"It's the subarctic," said Colt.

"Are you a scientist, too?"

"I'm a stock boy," he said. "How do you know each other?"

"We hitchhiked onto the same truck," said Dreadlocks. "Like, a thousand miles away from here."

"Wait a minute," Sunshine turned to me. "I thought you said you knew Merlin. From the alpaca farm. Where you were working?" She gestured to the wall behind me. "In Elma?"

"I did come from Elma," I said. "Yesterday. Before that, I came from even farther."

Dreadlocks waved a hand in front of her face as if she were erasing the entire conversation. "Wait," she said. "I came from Elma yesterday."

"Really?" I said.

"Where I was working. At the alpaca farm."

"I don't know who you are," Colt cut in, "or how you got your hair like that, or what kind of animal an alpaca is, but we" — he pointed the honey mustard between the two of us — "are going to Egg Island. Me and this girl here. Tell them about the map, Jules."

Sunshine forked a hotdog into her mouth and chewed, very slow.

"It's just a map," I said to Colt.

"That leads to a place only a few people in the world know about. And we don't know what we're gonna find, but we might be able to see through to another dimension. Or the flip side of the galaxy. Or the place we go when we die." He poked me with the mustard. "That's what I think it is," he said.

Dreadlocks laughed.

"Who'd you get your weed from?" she said. "Greg? Or Bryan? Must have been Bryan."

"Neither of them," said Colt.

"Egg Island," Sunshine interjected. "I've heard of this. Some cult from the sixties, right? The snowsuit one? My mom used to have these pamphlets about it that she kept with all her Woodstock stuff. *Truth Beyond the Ozone: What the Government Is Hiding. Get Home Posthaste, Before It's Too Late!* It's not real."

"I see," said Dreadlocks. "Do you get your snowsuit upon arrival?"

Colt dug his thumbnail under the mustard label.

"It's not the same thing," he said.

Then he looked down at me.

"Right?"

The never-ending flow of movement around us was becoming nauseating. I pressed my hands to my abdomen. I knew those titles, too. Those and several others, hidden in the jackets of records Mom hated so she wouldn't find them and throw them out.

"No," I said.

He tore off the label.

"Hey, man," Dreadlocks said to him. "Now no one's gonna know what flavour that is."

I closed my eyes and sucked in a deep breath to my stomach. When I opened them, the door had reappeared. Colt was on his way through it.

• • •

The bedroom was dark. I held a hand out to feel my way to the bunk, then collapsed, lay on my side, and kicked my shoes off at the heels. Bent my knees into my stomach. Smushed my face into the pillow so no one would hear my dumb sniffling. It was worse now than before, the aloneness. The hunger for sweetened condiments. Then the bunk shook.

"Hi," I heard from above.

"Mm."

"Okay?" she whispered.

I didn't respond.

"Okay," she said again.

I rolled onto my back. She poked her head over and looked down at me. Her long hair hung like black linguine.

"You still have cramps?" I asked her.

"No," she said.

I could hear the snot gurgling in both of our nasal cavities.

"We're all far from home," I said.

"Yes," she said.

"What's your name?" I asked her.

"Joo-Ha."

"Joo-Ha," I repeated.

Then I sat upright. Wiped my face with my towel.

"Joo-Ha, meet Julia," I said.

She looked out to the centre of the room.

"Who?"

I stood from the bed.

"Tomorrow will be better," I said. "For Joo-Ha and Julia both."

• • •

I followed the bouncing gold light of the candelabras down the long hall to the staircase at the end. The floorboards beneath my socks creaked with each step. At the bottom of the stairs, I passed through a dark room with furniture stacked and covered in white sheets, then, somehow, found myself in the entranceway once again. Ocean leaned back in a chair in front of the small desk, his hand resting in a bowl of microwaveable popcorn. Tinny sounds of gunshots and tires screeched from a small television with extended bunny ears.

"Excuse me," I said.

He dropped his feet down.

"Kia, shit," he said, spilling a handful of popcorn to the floor.

He crawled beneath the desk to pick up the kernels. Then popped his head back up.

"What's up, Julia?"

I pointed to the phone in the corner.

"Does that work?"

"You know, I've never actually seen someone use it before," he said.

I walked over to it, lifted the receiver. "There's a dial tone," I said.

"Huh." He smiled. "A treasure."

I sat on the bench. Used my pinky finger to wind the dial one number at a time. Finally, it connected. The phone rang once. The twins, on all fours, barked at the receiver on the wall. Twice. Mom swiped at them with a rolled newspaper. I hung up.

"Did it work?" Ocean asked.

I stood up from the bench. Walked back toward the entrance of the maze, glimpsing the screen as I passed his desk. Nicholas Cage, covered in blood. Smiling.

"Wrong number," I said.

. . .

"Colt," I whispered, knocking gently.

Soft snoring vibrated through the door. I knocked harder.

"Colt," I said again.

Then the thud of feet landing on the floor. The hardwood creaked, lock clicked. Colt opened the door a small crack.

"What do you want, Julia?" he whispered. "Or Elma, or Al. Or should I just call you Pinocchio?"

"Let me in," I said.

"I don't let in liars."

"Colt, I wouldn't lie to you."

"Yeah, that's what a liar would say."

"Please just talk to me. It's not like how it sounded."

He closed the door.

"I'm not wearing a shirt," he said. "I don't want you to see my nipples."

I pushed against the door with my shoulder until he moved out of the way. He backed into the middle of the room and stood with his hands tucked into his armpits.

"Colt, I've seen your nipples before."

"We were swimming. It's not the same."

"How was your pasta?" I said.

"I lost my appetite."

"You didn't eat anything?"

"No, I ate."

Someone rolled over on a top bunk, turning his back to us. Colt nodded in his direction. Then, to the door.

"Bryan's sleeping," he said.

"Yeah. Maybe we should get out of here."

"One of us should."

I looked down at my feet.

"Fine," I said. "Okay."

I backed out into the hallway. Colt leaned against the door-frame, still covering his chest.

"I just wanted to let you know," I said.

"Know what?"

"That I'm leaving in the morning. To go back."

"Back where? Home?"

"Yes."

"How you gonna get there?" he said.

"Find a bus station."

"You have money for a bus?"

"Yes, I have money for a bus."

He dropped his hands hesitantly, looking down at his nip-ples in the light of the hall. Then straightened his shoulders and neck and shook out his hair. Then he looked straight at me. At my eyes. In that tenderly murderous way that only he could. For one second, I felt light, a tuft of dust kicked up from the unswept floor. Then he shut the door. I stood there staring at the jackrabbit painted in the centre of it. Waiting. But eventu-ally, I knew I had to walk away.

Down another hall, I found a door I hadn't been through yet. There was a bear painted on it, stomping on a car someone had markered beneath its feet. It led down a flight of stairs and through a second door to the veranda at the back end of the house. There were no chairs, so I sat on the wood. Besides my breath and the shuddering wheat of the surrounding fields, it was completely silent. Until the sound of beating wings over-took it. A crow the size of a small dog swooped in from nowhere and took up a position on the rail beside me. Its head twitched and turned. It rustled its feathers. Dad had thought birds might be the ferries, the ones to carry us from here to whatever it was beyond here. Which was why they'd been able to adapt and survive all this time. All these millions and millions of years.

"Where did you come from?" I said to the crow.

It spread its swings as if it were about to fly off, but didn't. Just indicated the space around itself.

"Okay," I said. "I get your point."

XXIX

I ROLLED OVER in bed. The first hint of daylight weaselled through the curtains. I lifted my arm above my face. The pain was gone. The bruise was gone. Everything was as normal as could be, as if nothing had ever happened. That fox had never even existed. I curled my fingers in and out. Stretched my elbow. Punched the air. Then, from the bed above, I heard the soft turn of a page. I stood from my bed to find the saddest girl in the world upright and reading.

"Joo-Ha," I said.

"Morning," she said, without looking up from her book.

"Did you sleep?" I asked her.

She nodded once. Her eyes were bright and dry.

"Look," I said, and held my limb up in the air like it was a trophy. She looked at my face. Then my arm. Then turned back to her book.

"I know, right?" I said. "Like it was all a dream."

. . .

The mansion was still and quiet. No voices channelling spirits. No Ocean at the front desk. Upon opening the door to the veranda, however, I was met with the rhythmic screeching of the chair swing. Colt with his long legs, ringing in the new day.

"What are you doing up so early?" I said.

"I woke up. Can't a guy wake up without it being some big deal?"

"It's not," I said. "I was only asking."

"This doesn't have to be a big deal," he said.

"Okay."

"Good."

I set my backpack down at my feet.

"Colt, can I explain stuff to you?"

"Wait, Julia. Wait."

He stopped rocking. Wiped his hands against his jeans.

"I'm going to do something now," he said.

"Okay. What?"

He stood from the swing and stepped in front of me.

"Don't be scared," he said.

"Okay."

Several moments passed where all he did was blink a lot.

"What is happening?" I said.

"This," he said. Then some more nothing happened. Just blinking. Until finally he hunched forward, closed his eyes, and kissed me directly on the eyeball. He backed away very quickly after.

"Ow," I said, covering my eye.

He knocked his fist against his forehead.

"Sorry," he said.

"Did you just kiss my eye?"

"Yes," he said.

Another moment passed. Then he lifted my miracle arm and dropped it.

"Hope this works," he said.

"Hope what works?"

"We need to push the car to the gas station. It's three blocks away."

. . .

I sat in the driver's seat, right hand on the clutch, left hand on the steering wheel, while Colt pushed from behind, his grunting and bemoaning echoing off the empty road. Fresh bird droppings fell to the windshield, where old ones were already well-caked on. I looked up at the radiant light of the gas station sign ahead. As we crept closer, a stoplight above clicked to red. I leaned out the window. Colt was bent over, trying to catch his breath.

"We're almost there," I shouted. "You're doing great!"

A thousand butter knives flung from his eyes. Then we both looked up as the light clicked to green.

"Three, two, one," I screamed.

"MY NAME IS Julia Bermuda Tillerman. I'm eighteen years old.
I'm on my way to Egg Island to find my father, who's up there,
I believe, waiting for someone to come and bring him home."

"Bermuda?"

"Shut up."

"That's less believable than your age."

The fields stretched into infinity. A solitary silo. Hay bales
proliferating for miles. Chemtrails criss-crossing against the
troposphere. The enormous sky appeared to have ten different
weather systems moving from one horizon to the next to the
next.

"How long has he been gone?"

"What day is it today?"

"Let me think. If I was stocking pop the day we left, then
that day was a Thursday, because the pop comes in on the
second Wednesday, unless it's a month with thirty-one days,
in which case it sometimes doesn't come until the end of day
Thursday. So, it could have been a Friday."

"A month. Maybe more."

"And he's looking for an ozone hole?"

"Whatever it is that's up there."

I could feel Colt glancing over at me then. Could see it, too, in my periphery. Not in a way that needed me to look back at him. But in a way that needed me to remind him he was driving a car.

"Eyes on the road, Colt."

He turned his head forward.

"You know, people used to think God was up there, sitting on a cloud throne," he said. "And then we invented planes and saw that actually, there was nothing but more sky."

I rotated the map to our current perspective.

"Then, we started to think the guy was up in space, sitting on a nebulous throne. So, maybe one day, we'll invent galaxy planes and see that that's not true, either."

"You mean, like, spaceships?" I said.

He flicked his lighter.

"Let me see that map," he said.

He glanced over at my lap.

"There's nothing. For a long time. We just keep driving straight."

Colt stepped on the gas and overtook a plow. Out the window, a large hawk dove to the ground, then beat his way back up, the writhing silhouette of his lunch dangling from his talons.

XXXI

· · · · · · · ·

"DO YOU HEAR that?"

"No."

"Listen."

Colt squinted.

"You don't hear it?"

"No," he said.

"It's like, a knocking. What's a transmission? Could it be that?"

Colt listened.

"It's called your brain," he said. "Tricking you into thinking there's something wrong."

"Let's pull off in the next town."

"Julia, chillax."

"I need to use the washroom, anyway."

"There's an empty water bottle in the back."

"Find a spot in the next town," I said.

Wind beat against the doors and roof. Through the windshield, I watched as immense grey- and rose-coloured clouds hurdled one other, while behind us, there was just easy blue. Far back from the road, the very tiny figure of a person stumbled out the door of an unhitched trailer, waving their arms over their head. I turned in my seat and watched out the rear window until we were too far away to know if they really had needed help.

XXXII

THE FIRST TOWN we arrived in appeared to be abandoned. Houses were boarded up, school windows had been shattered. Graveyard grass covered the tombstones. A person on a bicycle biked slowly past a row of shops for lease. Only a library in the centre of town emitted any light.

"Who do you think's in there?" I said.

"The Pagemaster," said Colt.

I shivered.

"Don't you have to go, too?" I said.

"No."

I unbuckled, climbed out of the car, and walked toward the marble steps. Two gargoyles were perched on the ledge above the door. A cold wind brushed my bare arms and legs. I turned around.

"But you should try," I called back. "Just in case."

Colt rolled down his window.

"What?" he yelled.

"Just in case. You should use the washroom now."

"I have a wiener. I can go wherever."

"Please, just come in with me."

He groaned. But unbuckled his seatbelt. We walked up the steps side by side, and when he pulled open the heavy door, we were immediately thwacked with frigid air conditioning and blazing fluorescents. A single long table was placed in the centre of the room. At one end, a tall man in a yellow knitted cardigan layered over a pink knitted sweater sat arranging torn newspapers like a bird building a nest. At the other, two potato-shaped men, fuzzy and ashen, were positioned across from one another with a chessboard set in between. One used both hands to lift a single piece, straining as if it were as heavy as a five-pin bowling ball.

"Where are the books?" said Colt.

A lady in a purple parka with strips of duct tape along the seams dozed in a ratty armchair, the pushcart parked beside her bulging with plastic bags. The librarian behind the counter stared at nothing, doing nothing.

"Wait here," I mouthed to Colt.

"What?" he said.

The newspaper man looked up.

"Don't leave," I whispered.

"Go fast," he said.

I walked past the table and between two empty bookshelves toward the washroom.

"Checkmate," I heard the two potatoes chant in unison behind me.

Colt caught up.

"I'll just escort you," he said.

. . .

He waited outside the washroom. When I'd finished, I bent over the marble sink and splashed cold water on my face. Then leaned in toward the mirror. Sucked in my cheeks and raised my eyebrows to make waves of wrinkles across my forehead. Then released, poked at the puffs of baby fat that inflated when I smiled.

Colt opened the door a crack.

"What's taking so long?" he whispered.

I tore a paper towel, dried my face, and tossed it on the floor.

"Nothing," I said.

After leaving the washroom, we walked quickly toward the exit, not looking up yet still catching a whiff of the mould emanating from Newspaper Man's newspapers. When we reached the door, Colt pushed it open and rushed down the steps. Once he reached the car, he realized I wasn't behind him. Turned back around to find me still standing by the door.

"What now?" he said. "Let's go already."

"One sec," I said, turning back inside. In the entrance was a bulletin board covered in newspaper clippings and photos, some with handwritten info. Missing children, teenagers, a few adults. One girl, thirteen, hadn't been seen for ten years. She'd had long dark hair parted at the centre, wide brown eyes, and was last seen wearing a Monkees T-shirt. She'd kept a yellow woven bracelet tied to her right wrist. Had been her mother and father's baby. Below her photo was a sketch of what she might look like now. It was a bit like a horse. Colt opened the door.

"Julia," he said.

"Sorry," I said.

"What for?"

He looked at the board.

"Have you seen that horse?" he asked me.

A chair squeaked and echoed through the building. I looked over at the librarian, whose position hadn't changed in the slightest since we'd arrived.

"One more second," I said to Colt. Then walked over to the counter. I stood in front of the librarian and pointed to the phone. Without looking at me, she slid it forward. I picked up the receiver and listened to the dial tone.

"Three, two, one," I counted.

The phone rang four times and went to the machine.

"Hello?" I said after the beep. "If you're there, pick up."

A click and rustle on the other end.

"Juya?"

"Zenny! Good job. Is Mom home?"

"Juya! I miss Juya."

"I miss you, too, Zenny. Is Mom home?"

"Mom not here."

"Where is she?"

"Mom sad at Juya!"

"Zenny, listen. Is anyone there? Is Joan there?"

"My Joan come over later."

"Are you and Michael alone?"

"Yes."

"Zenny, you shouldn't tell people that you're alone. You shouldn't even be answering the phone if Mom isn't there."

"Juya said?"

"I know I said to pick up. But if you're all alone in the house, you should never answer the phone. Ever. Why did Mom leave you all by yourselves, anyway?"

Because their babysitter was in a library in the middle of the Twilight Zone.

"Never mind," I said.

"Juya! Coming home?"

"Not yet. But listen. Listen very, very carefully, Zenny. I have a very important job for you."

"Job?"

"Hang up the phone and when I call back, don't pick it up."

"Bye Juya?"

"Yes. Bye, Zenny. Hang up now."

"Okay."

I sighed, picturing the two of them staring at the phone, waiting. I dialled again. He answered on the first ring.

"Zenny, you aren't supposed to answer, remember? Hang up the phone, and when it rings, do not pick it up."

"Bye Juya?"

"Yes. Goodbye. Do not answer the phone."

"Do not answer the phone, Zenny!" Michael shouted in the background. Then a smack, and a scream.

"Juya!"

"Zenny, pass the phone to Mikey."

Mikey breathed heavily into the receiver.

"Mikey, hang up the phone."

There was a click. I called again. It rang four times. On the fifth it went to the machine, but by that point, I'd lost my words. Colt elbowed me in the back. I cleared my throat.

"Mom? It's me. I'm fine. Everything is fine, and I'll call you again soon. Don't be worried or anything. I'm with my friend."

Colt leaned over my shoulder and whispered close to the receiver.

"And I love you."

"And I love you," I said.

Then I hung up. Slid the phone back to the librarian fixed in her place far, far away.

XXXIII

"RUB MY SHOULDER," said Colt.

"What?"

"My right shoulder. It hurts."

"From what?"

"From driving across the whole entire universe."

I poked him in the shoulder. "Good?"

"Do it better."

I squeezed hard with my thumb and forefinger. He yelped, swerved.

"What the hell," he said. "Do it good. Seriously. I'd do anything for you."

He laughed at himself.

"I'd jump in front of a sawn-off shotgun for you," he said. "I wouldn't even have to think about it."

"Yeah, I know," I said.

To our left was a dam churning up a shallow river. I looked out the windshield, down at the lines on the road, woolly, like the paint was running. Then back up to the dam. Down to the road. At a tree that appeared to be sliding backward.

"I ran away from home once, before," Colt said.

"When?"

"A couple of years ago. My grandpa lost a testicle over it."

"Where'd you go?"

"Nowhere. I'd just got my licence, so I kind of stole the car. Like this."

"Why?"

"Because Grandma."

"What'd she do?"

"Got cancer and died. For no reason."

Ahead, a kid waved to us through the back window of a camper van. Colt waved back.

"So, you stole the car?"

"Yeah. My grandpa kept trying to tell me all this stuff about the afterlife, and cancer facts. Stuff I didn't care about. I kept saying to him, 'What the fuck are we going to do at Christmas? You can't bake. I can't bake. Neither of us knows how to make the tree look good. Or hang up that beautiful shiny stuff.' I tried. It didn't look beautiful. It barely looked shiny. Everything was all clumped together, and I couldn't even get the tree to stand straight. It was one of those fake ones that stays in a box all year. Like it takes a genius to get those to stand straight. Or a grandma."

"You just keep bending the thing until it works."

"Okay, well, I couldn't make it work. It was stupid as dog shit. So I took the car and drove away."

He reached for the map wedged between the cup holders. I opened it for him and folded it back on itself. Then looked back out the window. Fields upon fields. So much nothingness.

"What made you go home again?" I said.

"The street signs turned French. So I turned back and chopped down a tree. All by myself. I took an axe and chopped her down."

"The tree was a girl?"

"About as tall as you. I carried her all the way home on my shoulder, through the gas station, and up the stairs to the apartment. Then I took the other one, the dog shit one, carried it down the stairs, through the gas station, outside, and set it on fire."

"Outside the gas station?"

"The box of decorations, too. I set them on fire, too. Then I put up the real one, and it stood straight. And so we just had a naked tree in the apartment. Naked and dead, or dying, or whatever a tree becomes once you decapitate it."

"I guess it would be dead at that point."

"Yeah. It smelled good, for something that was dead."

He rested an arm along the window pane. Flicked his lighter uselessly against the wind. I wondered how many blades of grass it took to make a field. How many mice and seeds and dandelions we'd driven past at that point. How many ants.

"Maybe it isn't nothingness," I said.

"What isn't?"

Then a hiss, a clunk, and steam from the beneath the hood.

XXXIV

COLT STEERED TO the curb.

"What happened?" I asked him.

He unbuckled his seatbelt and opened the door. The car filled with cold air. He walked around to the front and placed both hands on the hood. Then he jumped back and yelped, blowing on his palms.

"Are you okay?" I yelled.

He waved his fingers at me through the windshield.

"Do it," he shouted.

"Do what?"

"The lid."

I stared back at him, confused.

"Pop the lid," he shouted again.

"How?" I shouted back.

He shook his head. Walked back around to the driver's side, leaned in, and pulled a lever beneath the seat.

"Like this," he snapped.

"Hey," I said, "it's not like I made the car break down. I told you I heard something."

"It's overheated."

"Okay. So we stop for a bit and let it cool down."

"It's not that simple," he said and slammed the door shut. He walked back around to the front of the car, lifted the hood, and stood hugging himself, rocking back and forth. I climbed out to join him. The heat from the car was a cloud of doom emanating from the black mess of engine. And other stuff. I had no idea what I was looking at.

"Do you know what you're looking at?" I asked him.

"Yes, Julia, I know what I'm looking at. I wouldn't be driving a car through the middle of nowhere if I didn't know what a car looked like."

He lifted some things and touched others with his fingertips. There were goosebumps on his arms. He stood straight again, stuck his hand out toward me. I reached to shake it. He dropped it to his side.

"What are you doing?" he said.

I shrugged.

"A sweater. Or T-shirt. Something I can use to get a grip."

I climbed into the back seat, unzipped my bag, and sifted through it to find my dirty, stolen, monogrammed towel. Then went back and handed it to Colt. He rubbed the grease from his fingertips and leaned into the car to unscrew something from something else. Then bent lower, examining the part. Stood straight and screwed a small lid back in place. Then held the towel back out without looking at me. I caught it as he let it go. Telephone wires buzzed above. A bird screeched over and over. Colt kicked the bumper.

"Quiet," he shouted. "Asshole bird."

"Don't call the bird an asshole," I said.

He let out a hard breath. I reached to touch his shoulder, but he stepped away.

"It's going to be okay," I told him.

"Really? Are you gonna fix it?"

"Someone'll come along eventually."

"I haven't seen anyone in a while."

He squatted down and picked up a stick, drew a circle, then another, slightly bigger circle. I thought he was drawing a snowman. Then, halfway through the third, even bigger circle, he stopped and whipped the stick at the road.

"Sorry," I said.

"What are you sorry for now?"

"I don't know. I've never seen you angry like this before."

"Yeah, well. You haven't been with me this entire time, have you."

I didn't respond.

"And you weren't with me my entire life before any of this happened either, were you?"

I shook my head no. Even though he wasn't looking at me.

"It's gonna be fine," I said again.

"Because you think I'm gonna fix this."

"What?"

He stood and turned to face me.

"You think I'm going to fix this. You think whenever anything goes wrong, it's okay, 'cause Colt's here to fix it. But once you don't need me, you're up and out the bathroom window."

Then he walked past me through the ditch and ran out into the field of corn sprawled out next to us.

"Where are you going?" I called after him.

"For a run," he shouted back, tucking his arms inside his T-shirt. He looked like the top half of an armless scarecrow, his head and shoulders bobbing off through the corn. Until eventually, he was too far away, and I couldn't see him anymore. Couldn't hear him, either.

. . .

I propped my legs up along the back seat picking stale Fritos crumbs from a half-eaten bag I'd discovered on the floor. Two cars and a truck had already passed without stopping. I started singing to myself. Quietly, then louder. "A Whole New World." The one that calmed down the twins when they were fighting.

Then a small black car appeared far down the road. I sat up. It got closer, and I jumped out of the back seat, waving. Then waving and jumping, then waving and jumping and shrieking as it sped past. I didn't stop until it reached the curvature of the Earth and descended. I looked back to the field. Still no sign of Colt. Half the sky was turning pink as night fell. Then a second car began to roll over the horizon.

I climbed onto the trunk and crawled to the roof. Stood on my knees and waved my arms above my head. When it got closer, I climbed to my feet. The metal whined beneath me. I called out, "Stop! Please!" again and again, then watched as it, too, passed and continued on, becoming another speck receding to the other side of the world.

I jumped from the roof of Colt's grandpa's stolen car and stormed out into the field, into the corn that loomed over my head, condensed in front of me, beside me. Behind me, somehow. It seemed I was shrinking into the pest I truly was, a terrible sister, daughter, vehicular passenger. I was probably

EGG ISLAND   141

destroying this crop, even, stomping around like this, crush-
ing some poor farmer's livelihood. I called out for Colt. No
answer.

I kept walking, in which direction I had no idea, until I
came across a clearing, small and circular. I walked up to the
edge of it. There were no footprints, no tire tracks. But on the
other side, protruding from the crop, the thick sleeve of a jacket
just like Dad's. Nylon, orange. Dirty, like it'd been trampled.
Or else like it'd been there for a while. Like the owner was
gone. Really gone. Never coming back for it.

I took a step closer. Dad in the crawlspace, pulling out his
old gear. Hockey pants and socks. Looking for the ski suit he
hadn't used since his twenties. *Help, Julia*, he'd said to me.
You're small. It must be tucked all the way in the back.

It's Labour Day, I told him. *What do you need all this junk
for?*

He didn't answer.

What happened to you, girl? he'd said instead. *What happened to my special assistant?*

Then, I heard a howl. I turned back, running, trying to
find some sign of a path to retrace, but couldn't. So I just went
opposite the way it seemed the howls were coming from. Finally,
the corn dispersed, and I could see the ditch, the car. I climbed
over to the front seat and rolled up the windows. Buckled the
seatbelt and locked the doors.

Colt hit the window beside me. I screamed.

"It's just me," he said.

I held both hands to my chest. Tried to breathe normally,
but I just kept coughing. My face was steeped in cold sweat.
Small traces of blood flecked my arms and thighs, scratched
from the brush.

"What the hell, Colt? Why were you gone for so long?" I yelled.

"Are you okay?" he asked. "You look bad."

I unbuckled the seatbelt and opened the door. Stepped out of the car, forcing him back into the ditch. Then I stood right in front of him and punched him in the arm as hard as I could. He laughed.

"Why did you do that to me?" I shouted.

"I just went for a run," he said.

"Yes, I know that you were running," I shouted again. "I want to know why you were running, and why you just left me here like that?"

"I was upset."

Bats zipped above our heads. I swatted the air frantically.

"I heard howling," I said.

"What kind of howling?"

"The coyote kind, or wolf. Can we go yet?"

"No."

I punched him again.

"What do you mean, no? What's even wrong with the car?"

"Stop punching me," he said. "It tickles."

"What's wrong with the car?" I said again.

"We need coolant. It's out, and if I keep driving without it, the car will explode."

"Really?"

"Yes."

Stars were starting to appear above. We could see our breath. Colt made a peace sign in front of his mouth, flicked his lighter, and pretended to smoke a cigarette.

"You wanna smoke?" he said.

I smacked the lighter out of his hand.

"Hey," he said, bending to pick it up. "Did anyone drive by?"

I shook my head no. Colt nodded.

"People can be jerks," he said.

I stepped out of the ditch. He crouched down beside me and placed both hands on the road.

"We're gonna get eaten by whatever that thing was," I said.

"Yeah."

Then he crawled forward on all fours and sat down in the centre of the road.

"Sorry I went on such a long run," he said.

"It's not about the run," I said. "What are you doing?"

He stretched his legs out and lay flat on his back.

"Come see this," he said.

"Colt," I said. "Get up."

"Oh, just do it, Julia," he yelled.

"Colt," I repeated. "There's a car coming."

. . .

The passenger window rolled down, and a young woman leaned over from the driver's seat.

"Do you need help?" she asked.

"Yes!" Colt exclaimed.

"Not you," she said to him. She pointed to me. "You. Do you need some help?"

"Me?" I said.

"We're toasted," Colt said. "We need some coolant."

She unbuckled her seatbelt, slowly. Then popped the trunk.

"I have a knife. Just so you know," she said, climbing out of the car, leaving the door open and dinging. As she met Colt in the tail lights, she raised her hand to show him the small Swiss Army pocket knife tucked against her palm. He held out his hands to show her nothing.

"All right," she said.

She leaned into her trunk and pulled forward a box of tools from the back. Opened it and handed him a container of lime-green liquid. Then took out a flashlight, which she turned on and pointed at my face. I held my hand up to block the light.

"How old are you?" she said.

"Eighteen."

She pointed the light at Colt. Then back at me. Then back at Colt.

"What are you guys doing out here?" she said.

Colt looked down at me.

"We're on our way to Egg Island," he replied.

She pointed the light back at me. I smiled.

"Now's your chance," she said to me. "If you need help, speak up."

"It's the truth," I said.

She pointed the light back at Colt. Held it there for a few moments. Until he began to pluck an air bass.

"Let's go see your car," she said.

. . .

Colt poured the contents of the container into the black hole as the woman held the light above. When he was done, he shut the hood, bounced around to the driver's side, reached in to start the engine, and let it rumble. Then twirled back around to face us, opening his arms for a hug. The woman held up her knife again, pointed at it with the light. Redirecting the hug to only me, he lifted me up, spun in a circle, then dropped me back down.

"Which way are you going now?" the woman said.

Colt pointed north.

"I guess you're sticking with me," she said. Then returned to her car. Colt and I climbed inside ours, buckled up, and watched her drive ahead.

Finally, we pulled away from the curb.

XXXV

· · · · · · · · ·

"WHAT IF WE'RE about to go die," I said to Colt.

"Then we'll be dead and we won't feel anything."

I rested my head against the window.

"I take care of my ants," Colt said. "To them, I'm this enormous man who could squash them all in one step. But I don't. I take care of them."

The headlight beams veered as Colt turned to face me. I sat up and reached for the steering wheel.

"Colt," I said.

He looked back at the road.

"Look," he said.

I waited for him to continue.

"What?" I said.

"No, look."

He leaned over the steering wheel. Bands of yellow and green light careened in front of us. I rolled down my window, stuck my head out. Watched them swell as the wind ate my face.

"People used to think this was God stuff, too," Colt said. "Before geophysics happened."

I pulled my head back in. "So, what you're saying is that there will always be a God-related mystery."

"And we'll be there to solve it," said Colt.

. . .

The next town was a void, the buildings scarce. Each was like a garage, square, metal, low to the ground. A group of bundled-up men stood smoking outside of one with a glowing white sign that read *BAR* in black letters. At an empty intersection with a stoplight hung in the centre, we pulled up beside our saviour's car. She waved goodbye, her blinker blinking. Then Colt rolled down his window. After a moment, she rolled hers down, too.

"I'm turning here," she said. "You guys know where you're going?"

"You know where we could find some food?" Colt asked.

She looked out her window.

"No," she said. "There's a motel, I think, two blocks that way. They might have a vending machine."

In the light of the headlights, I could see her looking past Colt, at me. Like she wanted to tell me one more thing. But couldn't say it out loud.

"Thanks for not stabbing me," said Colt.

She nodded, rolled up her window. We waved goodbye. The car turned, then dissolved where the streetlights ended.

The teensy old man at the motel led us to a room, rattling keys in his shaky hands. Every fraction of his face was wrinkled, his eyes teary behind thick, round glasses. The room was twenty-one dollars, and the bed was lumpy. The wallpaper mimicked the appearance of wood. Everything white was yellow, everything beige was brown.

"It's perfect," Colt sighed.

He released the armful of vending machine snacks onto the bed, then fell forward after them. I dropped my backpack to the floor and pulled a chair out from beneath a robust black desk, metal, like it belonged in a doctor's office. Colt reached for the remote on the nightstand, sat up, and turned on the small television set that sat on a crooked piece of wood screwed into the wall. The screen buzzed as it brightened.

"Let's see," he said.

He flipped through the channels. Fuzz, more fuzz, Arnold Schwarzenegger. Set the remote back down. Opened a bag of potato chips. The heat coming through the radiator smelled like burning paper. I looked over my shoulder at Colt. He looked at me. Then back up at the screen. Then back at me.

"Stop looking at me," he said.

I turned to face the desk, drummed my nails against the surface. Then opened the drawers. One black winter glove in the first, beneath which was a folded road map. I closed the drawer. Checked the lower one. Empty. I kicked its side and it echoed. I looked back at Colt. His eyes were red, though not blinking. Like he refused to miss a single frame of the movie. I couldn't blame him. I stood up, went over to the bed, and crawled up beside him with some nuts, the corn kind, and stretched out on top of the thin pink comforter. Leaned back against the wall. It wasn't long until his head had fallen to my shoulder, and the second the credits hit, he was asleep. I pulled the chip bag he was wearing like a mitt from his hand, then shrugged his head down to the pillow. Folded my side of the comforter over top of him.

I pushed all the food from the bed into the backpack, then sat back down at the desk. The top drawer squealed at first as I pulled it open. But Colt didn't move. I took out the map from inside, unfolded it halfway to the index, and searched the infinite list of tiny black words. Then flipped it back over.

Egg Island really was an island. Surrounded only by water and other distant, unidentified islands. No solid land in any direction for at least forty-five kilometres. No roads. I pulled my backpack over to my feet, dug out our map. It was folded the same way as the new one. Same thickness. I spread it open on top of the other one. Same height and width. Same title. It'd been there in the orphaned mittens and socks basket with all the other road maps, on the floor by the door, forever. That's where it had lived. What were the others for? Places farther away. Florida, maybe. I couldn't remember. Because they didn't lead anywhere he'd ever need to go.

But Colt was right. Right that it wasn't right. That it was missing things. A quarter of the index. And a publisher. I refolded both. Shoved the new one into the backpack beneath the chips. The original, I took to the washroom. Lifted the back of the toilet and dropped it into the water. In the dark, there was no way of seeing whatever it was that was making that cauliflower smell. But I was glad for it. Because the longer I stood there, the more all-consuming it became, the only thing my mind could grasp on to. That strange, decomposing funk.

I left the washroom and climbed back into the bed. Lay on my side, facing Colt's back wrapped in the covers, using the flannel as my own blanket. And left the television on. So when he woke again, he could have at least one happy start.

XXXVI

WHEN I OPENED my eyes, the television was off. I was buried beneath the comforter, too, while Colt was still sleeping next to me with the flannel stretched over his arms and chest. I slid out slowly from the bed and went to the washroom. Tilted the lid back to check the map was still there. It was. Then I crossed back through the room, opened the front door, and stepped barefoot into the cold morning. The air was dry, the clouds orange and blue. Strange hot-pink weeds surrounded the base of a telephone pole like Lite-Brite pegs. For the first time ever, I felt very, very far away.

Colt lumbered through the door, still holding the flannel around his shoulders.

"We must be close," he said. "Considering how insanely freezing cold it is here."

I looked down at my legs, goose-bumped below my jean shorts.

"You know," I said, "Terry Fox was just over halfway to reaching his goal when he stopped. But he'd done like, five thousand and something kilometres. You and me, we've only travelled like half of that."

"So?"

"So, he wasn't even close. He lived his entire life before he even started that run, and he ran so far past the start of it. But he was still so far from the end."

Colt looked out beyond the parking lot to the hills of brown grass covered in permafrost and nodded.

"You're gonna need pants," he said.

. . .

The motel restaurant smelled like lemon disinfectant and fryer oil. Céline Dion played from a radio behind the cash register. At one of the tables, an elderly couple sat in silence with milk and toast set between them. The woman handled a pill organizer. Pushed the pills, one at a time, toward her husband, who received them with unbending arthritic hands. At another table, a man in a red plaid jacket with a matching hat studied a map from behind his spectacles, a mug held beneath his chin.

Our breakfast arrived: two plates of eggs and honeydew melon.

"Can we get some ketchup?" Colt asked the waitress.

"You can," she replied, in a very deep voice. "But, may you?"

"May I what?" he said.

"Have ketchup, please?" I said to the waitress.

"Yes, you may," she said. Then turned and set the caddy of condiments from the table next to ours in front of me. Colt reached across the table, took the ketchup bottle, and squeezed a spiral around his entire plate. I took a bite of melon.

"How much money is left?" he said through a mouthful of eggs.

"We'd have to count," I said.

"'Cause we need to pay for the food, and we need gas," he said. "Do you know how to figure out the scale thing on a map?"

I moved some eggs around with my fork. "No."

"Give it to me," he said.

"Why?"

"Because maybe I can remember if I look at it. I took a geography class once."

I pushed back my chair, bent beneath the table where my bag sat between my feet, and pulled the zipper. Counted to ten. Then zipped it shut.

"I don't have it," I said.

"Yes, you do."

"No, Colt. I don't. It's not in here."

The old man at the other table began to hack, then spat a mass of phlegm into his cup of milk.

"So, we left it in the room," said Colt. He stood. "I'll go back right now before the maid shows up."

"I don't think any maid's going to be showing up anytime soon. Just eat your breakfast."

Colt looked over his shoulder at the man in plaid sitting behind us.

"He looks like he knows his way around here," he said. "I'm gonna go ask him."

"Ask him what?"

"How much farther to Egg Island."

"Colt, no," I started. But he'd already gone to the other table.

"Excuse me," Colt said to the man.

He lowered his spectacles.

"Hi there," he replied. "Good morning."

"Good morning to you," said Colt. "I see you have a map."

The man replaced his spectacles on his nose, looked at his map, then looked back up at Colt.

"Would appear so," he said.

"We're trying to get to Egg Island," said Colt. "Do you know it?"

The man looked back down at his map.

"Sure," he said, tapping a spot with a teaspoon.

Colt looked back over at me. Gave me a thumbs-up.

"Great. What's the best way to get there?"

"Probably boat."

"You can't drive a boat on land, sir," said Colt.

The man gestured for Colt to lean closer.

"Nothing more past here, son. No more roads. You'd need an off-roader, maybe. But then you'd need a boat. Boat that's good in ice."

Colt straightened.

"Our map doesn't look like this. It doesn't have all these holes. It has a road. I just don't know where it begins because I didn't see any signs when we were driving in last night."

"Those holes are water," said the man. "Water and space. Sounds like your map isn't true."

"Well, what if it's your map that's untrue?"

The man smiled.

"I been working in these parts a long time. Only way out's the way you came in."

I looked down at my plate. Held my breath and covered my face with both hands. Dad in the backyard with a parabolic microphone. Arm around my shoulder. Holding an earbud next to my head. Telling me one day, hopefully, he'd take me on a trip to Mars. He'd been saving up the money. We'd get ice cream on the way. Colt sat back down in his chair.

"Julia," he said.

I didn't lower my hands.

"You heard that?"

Then I did. And picked my bag up, rushed out of the restaurant. To the parking lot and toward the car. The day still hadn't started to thaw. Probably, it never would. I looked up at the icy sky and wished I could be as petrified as everything else in this place we were in. But I couldn't be. Not right away, at least. I'd have to stand still in place a little while longer.

"Hey," Colt called after me. "Why are you being crazy?"

"Don't run out on that bill, Colt," I yelled back. "Go pay the lady."

He walked over.

"It's okay," he said.

"What do you mean, it's okay?" I cried. "Pay her."

"I mean, it's okay," he said. "Think about it. It took us all the way here, that map. How could it take us all the way here and then just stop working?"

"You heard the man, Colt," I said. "People don't go there."

"Maybe that guy tells everyone to turn back. Maybe it's his job to sit at that table, in the last restaurant at the end of the last road, and tell people to go back, so no one may ever go on to see what's really up there."

"Colt," I said. "You need to go pay the lady now."

"Maybe he even met your dad."

I looked up, directly at the sun. So faint I didn't need to squint. Colt stepped toward me and turned my head away from it. Wiped my face with the sleeve of his shirt. It smelled sweet, like ketchup and melons.

"Maybe Terry Fox kind of knew all along," he said. "That he wouldn't make it across the whole country. But he still ran. He ran as if he was gonna go all the way. And in the process, he raised —"

"Colt, please." I reached into my backpack and pulled out the money. "Just go."

"I can't do that," he said.

"We can't just keep stealing eggs from people," I said, sobbing.

He looked past me at the road. Then stepped back, brushed all the hair from his face, and walked around to the driver's side of the car. Opened the door and leaned his elbows on the frosty roof. After a few moments he got in and started the engine. Rolled down the passenger side window.

"Get in," he said. "It's warm."

"No."

"Come on," he said. "You're beginning to look like Gorgon Heap."

"Hey."

"You're turning purple."

I looked down at my bare legs. Quivering and purple.

"I don't know what I'm doing," I said.

"Look," he said, "I don't know what I'm doing, either, all the way up here in the subarctic region of Northern Canada. With some girl whose name may or may not be Julia who I met at my grandpa's gas station barely a week and a half ago, on either a Thursday or a Friday. But what I do know is that my name is Colt. And I'm not going to leave you here. So, please" — he pushed open the passenger door — "get in the car."

I looked back at the diner.

"We didn't pay the bill," I said.

"We need that money for pants."

I looked back up at the sky. The moon was still out, too. It looked the same as the sun.

"Jules, we kind of have to go. Fast."

The restaurant door opened, and the waitress stuck her head out. Then started waving and hollering at us. I climbed into the car, tossed my backpack over the seat. Colt shifted into drive, and I closed the door. He pulled toward the street, and I felt the car accelerate, speeding. I buckled up. Leaned my head against the fogged window. Closed my eyes.

We drive for days, into weeks, stopping to panhandle, steal more food. We sleep in the car, but sometimes Colt drives through the night. When we end up back at the gas station where we met, he says goodbye, and I continue on foot, back the way I came. I never see Colt again. I walk for an entire day, and when I reach my house, I sit on the step outside for a while before Michael and Zen realize I'm there and start yapping at the window. Mom comes running, opens the door, and I stand up. She grabs my shoulders and looks me up and down and doesn't cry, because of the shock, I guess. Then she smacks me over the head and pulls me into the house, where she hugs me and sits me down on that old eggplant-coloured sofa and doesn't let me get up until I explain myself, which I can't. Dad sits beside me with his arm around me the entire time. I tell him, *It's going to be okay. You were right all along.* He's quiet. Michael and Zen paw at my feet. That night, I have a long, hot bath, and I put on clean pyjamas with Christmas trees all over them, and eat an enormous bowl of macaroni and hot dogs off a TV tray, and Mom keeps finding reasons to come over to me, to touch my hair or kiss my forehead. Dad is still quiet. After a few days, it's like I never left. I babysit the twins again. Soon, I go back to school. Months pass into summer, I get a part-time job in a hair salon, cleaning. The ladies let me watch them cut hair sometimes, and I go home and practise on old dolls, and on the twins. I babysit the twins more. One spring day I graduate high school, and that summer I practise cutting hair on myself. It doesn't turn out great. But the ladies give me a chair for kids' cuts. Mom moves out, moves in with Joan. Dad converts the garden shed into his private office. Soon stops coming into the house altogether. Me and the twins are alone a lot. Sometimes I pay the rent. I take the twins to school, cut the gum out of little kids' hair, come home, help the twins with homework. Years pass, and they start sleeping in beds, cushions on the floor no longer. Then, the twins are old enough to go live on their own. I go out back to the shed to tell Dad. But when I knock, there's no answer. I look under the door, through the gap in the bottom left panel, but see nothing. There's no one there. I wonder if there ever was, even, or if it was all just a thing I told myself. A thing that was never true. Still, I'm all alone in the house now, and it's too quiet. I go to a bar one night for a birthday party. I meet a kindhearted man, and I let him come and live in the house with me. One day he gets down on one knee in front of *Wheel of Fortune* and asks me to marry him, and I say yes, even though the answer was "a basket full of fresh fruit." Not much changes. Soon, I have a baby, and I love the baby. But the baby gets lonely with just me, so I make it another baby to play with. Eventually, the babies both need haircuts. The babies get older every day, and my body starts to look like an old banana peel. My husband kisses me, but he, too, has become overripe. He begins to look like an old

pear. Eventually, the babies turn into adults who move far away
and visit on holidays. They have babies, too. I give the babies'
babies haircuts, until my hands get too shaky to hold scissors
anymore. One morning, my old pear has a heart attack while
sitting across from me in our favourite breakfast joint and dies.
His head falls flat on the table, and our pills jump and scatter
all over the floor. I bury him a few days later. Then I start to
forget things. First, the way home. Then the names of all the
babies. One day, the twins visit me, and they're also rather ripe
by now. I ask them where my backpack is. They don't know
what the hell I'm talking about. Neither do I. I don't remember
Colt. I don't remember his grandpa's car, or the Milky Way,
or Baby Lake. The motels, the sticky diners, driving through
the endless prairies like travelling through space. I forget the
colours, the view to the other side. I forget Egg Island. My
head becomes empty, and so does my heart. Then I forget how
to walk, and then eat. And very quickly I forget how to live.
They bury me a few days after that, beside my old pear. We
compost, side by side, in our coffins six feet underground, six
blocks from the house I grew up in. Never to find proof that,
in the end, this could all be meaningless.

"Wake up," said Colt. "You're missing this."

XXXVII

THE CAR HAD stopped. Bison, one mother, two calves, blocked the road ahead of us.

"Get out," I told Colt.

He didn't move. His eyes were fixed on the giant marble eye of the mother, our small, red rectangle reflected somewhere inside. I unbuckled my seatbelt. Opened the door, climbed out of the car, and went over to his window.

"Colt," I said, knocking on the glass.

He snapped out of it.

"Get back in the car," he said.

"I want to drive," I said. "I need to learn. Now."

The mother snorted and stomped her front leg on the road.

"Get out," I said again, tugging at the handle.

He unlocked the door, and it swung open, knocking me backward. Then he moved over to the passenger seat. I took his place and shut the door.

"Don't move," he said.

I started the engine. He reached over and turned it back off. Took the key.

"Wait," he said. "As your teacher, I'm instructing you to wait."

Soon, the animals began to move. We followed the seesaw of their colossal brown heads as the mother led the way across the road. With the final swish of the second calf's tail, Colt placed the key in the cupholder between us.

"How do I do this again?" I said, restarting the engine. But didn't wait for an answer. I turned the wheel and stepped on the gas. The car cut across the road diagonally, and I hit the brake. Colt shifted the gear into reverse and put a hand on the wheel. Turned it away from himself, then let go, and shifted back into drive. I gassed again. We pivoted in the opposite direction.

"Keep going," he said.

And I did. I swerved until we were moving straight. The road out looked like some infinite river, with steady, slight crests, as though it'd just been left behind in the wake of some other two kids driving an old shitcan car, starting over from the top of the world. Colt reached beneath me and pulled on a bar that jerked the seat forward. Like I was a puzzle piece he was shifting into place. The speedometer went up, and up. Until Colt said slow down, and I let off the gas a bit. He didn't bother asking me why. Just helped. Made room for his own legs, and this time, he kept his eye on everything.

XXXVIII

WE WEREN'T IN a town or a village. There were no other roads in sight except the one we were on, the one we thought we'd been on before the motel. So the context in which we found the antiques store was nonexistent. Colt helped guide the steering wheel as I pulled to the shoulder. I turned off the engine. The tinkle of wind chimes in what was otherwise a sphere of silence leaked through the windows.

"I don't remember this," he said.

"Maybe we missed it in the dark."

We opened the doors. The building was a log cabin, the logs uneven in length. Strings of lights were strung over window panes, door panes, single kitchen table chairs, and plastic snowmen, all leaned against the outer walls. Gnomes, pumpkins strewn about. A boxing bag. Hockey sticks. It looked like a booby trap.

"Doesn't seem like something we'd miss," he said.

There was no path to the entrance. No parking or grass, either. Just brown space from all sides. So we walked through space. A busted carriage wagon with a bowling-ball-sized hole in the centre was parked in the middle of things. As well, a fake Venus de Milo. I knocked on the hard, hollow head.

"She's pretty," said Colt.

The door was so heavy it took both of us to pull it open. Its hinges screeched like a bunch of dying chickens. Inside, just stuff, floor to ceiling. And ceiling to windows. And floor to walls. A path big enough for one tiny person at a time began at the welcome mat we stood on and led onward to who knows where. I looked up at Colt slouched beneath a horde of mistletoe.

"Nothing surprises me anymore," I said.

"Just lead the way."

I started down the path. Behind me, Colt ducked, turning sideways where his shoulders wouldn't fit between shelves of dust-covered teapots and empty glass beer bottles, until we came upon a space devoted to racks upon racks of overstuffed clothing. I pressed my palms together in a diver's pose, trying to choose an entry point. Then a tap on my shoulder. I turned around. Colt was wearing a *Scream* mask and holding the sides of his face. Made a sound like he was gargling mayonnaise.

"Do you want to die, Julia?" he hissed.

"Kind of," I said.

He lifted the mask.

"I don't think anyone's here," he said. "I don't even think this place is open."

I listened. Nothing but the wind chimes. I turned back to the rack beside me and began unearthing clothing from the Titanic. Long silk dresses stitched with billions of beads, velvet vests. I pulled out a pair of wool trousers the colour of dirt and held them up to Colt's waist, over top of the torn belt loops of his grimy jeans. I couldn't tell which pair of pants smelled more like soup.

"Put these on," I told him.

He took them from me and proceeded to undress right where we stood. I continued to dig through the rack, through more trousers, skirts, ponchos. Until I found a pair of red corduroy pants sized for a puny waist.

"Okay, I got pants," I said, tugging them loose. "Let's get out of here before someone comes."

"Wait," he said.

I turned around. He was buckling his studded belt around the waist of the wool trousers, which sat all the way above his belly button. The cuffs fell just below his knees. A Hawaiian-print shirt tucked into the front. Red Wonder Woman cape on top. He pulled the mask back down.

"Help me find a mirror," he said.

I picked up his jeans from the floor and shoved them into his hands while shooing him back down the path. As we walked, I couldn't see anything beyond the walls of stuff immediately beside me and the Colt immediately in front of me.

"See anyone?" I whispered.

"No," he said.

"Lift your mask."

He raised the mask from his face.

"No one," he said. "Just fake people."

"Fake people?"

Between a bookshelf of cassette tapes and a bookshelf of shelving wood, I could see a line of scarecrows stood in front of a line of naked mannequins.

"Probably to deter thieves," Colt whispered. "And crows."

"I don't like this," I said. "Keep going."

"Look."

He leaned over a stack of china plates on the left, pulling a large, tubular sack from out behind. Then scanned the surrounding area. On the other side of the path, behind a ripped garbage bag stuffed with camouflage gear, was a pyramid of tin pots. He picked one off the top.

"Perfect," he said.

Then the pyramid collapsed.

"Go, go, go," I said, pushing against his back. We pressed on as fast as we could through the path, Colt knocking more shelves and low-hanging birthday decorations as we went. When we reached the welcome mat, we paused again to listen. Wind chimes.

"See," whispered Colt. "There's no one here. Hence the fake people. They're working."

"Don't say hence," I said, and pushed him to the door. We hurtled back through space, back to the car, Colt's cape flapping behind him. I climbed into the driver's seat, Colt, the passenger's. He tossed the sack and pot, plus his jeans, into the back. I started the engine. He took the wheel with one hand.

"Gas," he said.

We skidded onto the road.

"What's with the pot, Colt?" I shouted.

"You can cook with pots. Pay attention to the road."

I was driving in the centre. I swerved right, then left.

"I can't do this," I yelled. "Stop the car."

"You're the one driving," he said.

I hit the brake. Colt already had his arm across my chest to hold me back.

"It's okay," he said. "It's all a part of learning."

"Whiplash?"

"Panicking. When you're panicked like that, do everything opposite to the way you think you should in the moment."

He turned the wheel and, together, we slowly straightened out. He kept his hand on top of mine, and we drove a little farther up the road, then pulled to the side. Turned off the car.

"What's that other thing back there?" I said.

He turned in his seat. Then back around.

"That's a tent," he said.

"A pot and a tent?"

"Yes. We're going to set up camp."

"And what, hunt?" I said. "We're in the absolute middle of nowhere. There's no one, nothing. Nowhere."

"There's an antiques store."

"I think we should figure out where that cornfield is. Follow the road back the same way we came."

"And I think it's a sign that somehow we ended up someplace new in a land with supposedly only one road. Maybe this is the way your dad went."

I dropped my hands from the steering wheel. I didn't agree with him. I didn't see a sign in any of this. I saw us, buried in the snow that was about to fall any second, freezing, then thawing and mouldering in spring, shedding all the matter from our bones, attracting rats and mountain lions and birds, who'd shred up our clothing and hair to use for their nests. And then time plus wind covering us in dirt, burying our skeletons to be picked up two hundred years from now by some glacier that'll come sliding along and drop us off on the ridge of a mountain hundreds of miles away from here, where we'll be discovered by some mountaineering hiker guy when he gets his ice pick stuck in one of our skulls one day.

But also, what was beside me. Another person who I really, truly wanted to believe.

"How much longer do you think this car has left to live?"

"Three days."

. . .

We had a total of thirty-two dollars and seventy-five cents left. I shook the plastic bag, trying to break apart the coins to make more. Outside, Colt filled the tank. I shifted the backpack in my lap to nudge the map stuffed in the bottom into view. In the mirror I could see the side of Colt's head bobbing to music only he could hear. I plucked the map closer and tried to open it within the bag. Just enough to try to find us. The town we'd just come from, the cornfield. Then the nozzle clunked. I closed the bag over. Colt hit the roof of the car two times.

"Go ahead," I called.

He came around to the window. "You coming?"

I handed him the money. He reached through and took it.

"You trust me with all of this?"

I shrugged. He shrugged back. Then he turned toward the station. I watched him walking away out the back window. Until he stopped and looked back. I turned forward. Watched in the mirror until his cape coiled around the door. Then opened the map halfway on my lap. Once I found the last town we were in, I found the road we must have ended up on, taking us farther west. Another sixteen kilometres and we could turn back south. I buried the map again. Then got out of the car.

. . .

Colt was standing in front of the refrigerators. I went over beside him.

"That's good stock work," he said, looking them up and down.

"What flavour should we get? Orange?"

"We're not here for Fanta. We need water. Grab those two big bottles at the bottom and meet me at the counter."

He started off down the aisle stocked with non-perishables. I pulled the water from the fridge and followed. As Colt stacked cans of beans in one arm, I shifted the water to one hand and picked up a bag of marshmallows, a box of raisins. A can of green peas. Carried it all to the counter. He picked up the can of peas, examined it, and set it back down. Then took the raisins and walked them back to their spot on the shelf.

"We don't have enough for those," he said.

"We don't have two extra quarters?"

"Trust me. We're gonna need those quarters."

He pulled the money bag from the pocket of his trousers and counted out loud as he placed the coins on the counter. The clerk, a tall teenaged boy with a mess of blond hair and a lip ring, slid each coin, one at a time, into his palm, also counting out loud. Once they were both finished, the clerk flicked open a brown bag.

"That your car?" he said to Colt while filling the bag.

"Yeah."

The clerk nodded. Colt nodded, too. They both shook out their hair.

"Cool," said the clerk.

He pushed the bag forward on the counter. Colt picked it up with one hand and hugged it against his hip, the cape bunching up underneath it. I picked up the bottles of water, but he took them from me to carry, too.

"I got it all," he said.

"Why?" I said.

"Tell him what your dad looks like."

I looked at the clerk. Then back at Colt.

"He's got hair around his ears. Bald at the top, kind of."

"Don't tell me, tell him."

"Usually he wears a hat to cover it up," I said to the clerk. He shrugged.

"I see a lot of dudes," he said.

I nodded. Colt was rebalancing the bag slipping from his grip.

"Give it to me," I said, but he moved out of the way.

"I said I got it all," he said.

Then he walked ahead of me, backed up against the door to open it.

"This included. I got this also."

"See you around," the clerk called after us.

"See you around, too," Colt called back.

• • •

Once we were back on the road, I took up the corduroys I'd wedged between the cup holder and the seat and pulled them on over top of my shorts. One leg up on the dashboard at a time. Buttoned up the eight buttons that led to my ribcage. They were warm. A bit brittle. But warm.

"They fit," I said, watching for the upcoming right turn.

XXXIX

SOON I'D GUIDED Colt off the paved road and onto a dirt one with many holes, which he manoeuvered the car around as if we were inside a video game. Eventually, the road faded to two thin tire tracks, then to grass, then disappeared completely. That was when we stopped. We climbed out and found ourselves in a great green field, empty save for one tree that was short, with long branches extending out like an umbrella. Its leaves covered only one side, perfectly divided it right down the centre. Far off, train tracks wove between distant hills. I looked down at my pants. The bottom halves flared out in foot-wide bells.

"Did you know that bell bottoms were originally meant as practical uniforms for sailors?" said Colt.

"No," I said.

He opened the back door and pulled out the sack from the antique shop. A dark-green canvas bag with a drawstring. He loosened it, dumping out an assemblage of poles and more green canvas onto the ground.

"Then along came Sonny and Cher."

He picked up the corner of the fabric.

"What now?" I said.

"You don't build a tent by staring at it."

I took up one end of a pole, sending the other in his direction. He fed it through the loops in the fabric until it came out the other end, where he jammed it into the ground. I did the same. Together, we'd built half a triangle. Once we'd built the other half, he crawled inside the tent and buttoned up the door. On the back wall was a window flap, from where he called out to me. I went around to the other side. His eyes and forehead filled the entire hole.

"We'll need a password," he said. "Owl-eyed eagle will work."

"How about leopard-skin donkey?"

"Owl-eyed eagle is better."

I went back around to the front and slapped at the canvas door flap, as if to knock.

"Password?" said Colt.

"Owl-eyed eagle."

He unbuttoned the flap.

"The woodpecker has landed," he said.

"Why'd you change it?"

"That's the authorization."

"Isn't that what a password's for?"

"A password is for authentication. After the authentication, you need the authorization. Have you never used a tent before?"

"Okay. Can I come in, then?"

"Start over."

I forced my way through. He moved to the side, then rebuttoned the door behind me.

"Next time, be prepared," he said.

I pulled my knees into my chest. It seemed bigger on the inside than outside, like it was a real room.

"It's warm in here," I said.

"It'll be even better once we insulate."

"Kind of smells weird, though. Like cheese. Do you smell it?"

"Isn't it enthralling?" he said. "Think about the explorers who have sat right where you're sitting. Strategizing survival tactics. Writing letters home on tree bark."

"Or Boy Scouts threading macaroni necklaces."

He gazed around the tent like he was admiring a castle.

"And now, me. And you. Us. Building our own safe house."

Then he crawled forward and unbuttoned the door.

"We must make a fire before darkness falls."

. . .

We set the fire beneath the umbrella tree. I sat close to the embers, wearing all of my clothes to keep warm, while Colt cooked over the flame. Once the food was hot, he came and sat close to me. Spread his cape over our laps and held out four sticks.

"There were at least five racks of spoons at that antiques store," I said. "Tiny spoons from all over the world."

I tried to brush the dirt from my sticks using the sleeve of my sweater. But it was too dark to see the dirt good enough. And Colt'd already started in on the mixture of beans and corned beef in the pot. So I set the sticks between my fingers like chopsticks the same way he had. As I went for a scoop, they flicked from my grip.

"Here," he said.

He placed his own sticks behind his ears and helped to set up mine again. Then, hand over hand, lifted the food to my mouth. Miraculously, it tasted almost okay.

"Hey," I said. "This works."

"It's my grandpa's favourite."

He scooped another stickful to my face, then one to himself.

"Where did you learn how to use chopsticks?" I said.

"Where do you think?"

I thought about it.

"School?"

"Yeah. In chopsticks class. That's where I learned."

"Your grandpa?"

"No, in school. Ken taught me. His family was from Australia. He used chopsticks to eat his lunch every day. I thought it'd be a good skill to have, so I asked him to teach me and he brought me a set. I practised with him until I was a master. It didn't take long."

He took another bite. I readjusted the sticks between my fingers.

"This reminds me of this man I met," I said. "He was like, two hundred, maybe. He said he'd been wandering around for so long that he didn't know how old he was anymore. Or his own name. He just forgot it. He had a book and a small potato sack thing he used to carry charcoal he'd collected from train tracks. And he used the charcoal to draw pictures. He drew my picture on the back of some farm truck."

"Sounds like Ken," said Colt.

"I mean, the tent. And the person or people who might've also used the tent before. And eating like this. And those train tracks way over there. All of it, together."

I dropped my sticks again while pointing them out at the tracks. Felt for them in the shadows of the tree branches that stretched and moved across the ground like the limbs of a dancing giant. Colt gave me his.

"Most people will tell you it's all in the pointer finger," he said. "But I say it's in the thumb. Try again."

I picked up two beans. Colt opened the bag of marshmallows and stuck one to each end of two other, longer sticks he had at the ready beside him. Handed me one, then stood to roast his own marshmallow above the flames, turning it in slow, deliberate intervals. I set down the pot. Reached forward and stuck mine directly in the centre of the fire. Within seconds it was ablaze. A comet on a stick. I held it up to the sky.

"Caution," said Colt.

I lowered the torch directly in front of my face. The flame was still growing, blue, goo starting to slip.

"Blow it out," he said.

In the light of the fire, I could see Colt's face change. To that way again, like he'd forgotten what he was doing. He'd forgotten his own stick completely, and his marshmallow had melted right off. I brought the fire closer. Its sharp heat one twitch away from the tip of my nose and chin. I could hear it. It sounded like a rush. I opened my mouth as wide as possible.

Next second the stick'd been smacked from my hand and I was knocked over onto my back. Colt squatted over me, pinning down my shoulders.

"What are you doing?" I shouted. "Get off of me."

"No way, psycho."

"Get off," I shouted again, pushing back.

He let go of my shoulders but sat back on my shins. I tried to squirm out, to kick him, but he was too heavy. So I just swiped my hands at his face instead. Until he grabbed my wrists.

"You can't mess with fire like that, Julia," he yelled. "It's an incredibly powerful force."

"I know that," I yelled back, still trying to swipe, but really just wiggling my fingers and torso. He wouldn't let go. Even after I'd stopped. I tried to speak calmly.

"You can let go now. Please. And thank you."

"Your manners won't work on me," he said. "What were you trying to do?"

"I was just messing around."

"It takes a lot of training and skill to be able to eat fire. I can't do it yet."

"Can you let go of me now, Colt?"

He released my wrists, but not my legs. We stayed like that for a while. Still, he wouldn't change his face back to normal.

"What would I have done?" he said.

Beside us, the fire seemed to be growing brighter. Then we both realized the fire was supposed to be behind us, and the burning stick Colt'd tossed had begun to pick up whatever grass and leaves were surrounding it. He stood, pulling me up with him, and pushed me behind himself. Then started kicking dirt at the flames. They were spreading fast, creeping up the base of the tree. I picked up the pot and threw whatever was left inside of it onto the ground, which did practically nothing. Then dumped the bottle of water. A small sizzle, as the dirt Colt was kicking turned to mud. I started kicking it, too.

When we'd finally put it out, he picked up the bottle. Shook it over his mouth. Then handed it back without looking at me.

"One left," he said.

The dancing giant tangoed above.

• • •

I buttoned the door flaps down to where Colt's feet stuck out at the bottom. We'd spread whatever clothes we weren't wearing across the floor of the tent. He handed me the cape.

"What about you?" I said.

He crossed his arms over his chest and closed his eyes like a vampire resting in his coffin.

"Soon our inner thermal energy will warm the space around us."

The space around us smelled like burned grass. I lay down on my back.

"This reminds me of a woman I met who lives in a motel."

Colt opened one eye.

"What part?"

"The blanket."

I actually meant the smell.

"She used a cape for a blanket?"

"No. A tiger."

Colt was quiet. I raised my head. His eye had closed again. I lay back down and tucked myself beneath the cape. The walls of the tent shivered. I wiggled closer, stretching the cape to cover Colt, too. As much as possible, anyway. Warm puffs of air whistled from his nose through my hair while a train whistled from far away. Above, the window flap had come undone in the wind. Two white stars like bullet holes bore down on us. I could hear Colt's heartbeat. And I could hear the train getting closer. I could hear the wheels chugging, and the shrill friction of metal.

"I won't ever do that again," I said.

He didn't answer.

I was asleep before the train had even passed.

XL

· · · · ·

I WOKE UP to explosions. Bombs being detonated, or a firing squad. It was only just light, and I was alone in the tent. I sat up, panicked, and called out for Colt. Another blast. I covered my ears, squeezed my eyes shut. Tucked my head between my knees. Stayed like that for what felt like many, many minutes. Until nothing happened. It'd stopped. I raised my head, lowered my hands. Crawled toward the door. My fingers were shaking as I struggled with the buttons. I pulled back one flap, just enough to see. Far in the distance, beyond the tree, Colt was standing with hands on his hips, cape around his neck billowing in the morning breeze. I crept out from the tent. Everything was as it had been the night before. The car, the fire pit. Ash topped with frost. No shrapnel anywhere that I could see. I hugged myself against the cold. Our thermal energy had really worked.

"Colt," I shouted.

He didn't turn around. So I walked toward him in only my socked feet. Once I was a few feet away, he knelt down on one knee. I could hear the flick of his lighter. Then he stood, took three giant steps backward and collided right into me. A sudden blast burst from where he'd just been. I dropped to my knees and covered my head. He bent down beside me.

"You almost blew my coronaries," he said. "Why are you sneaking up on people?"

I looked forward to where he'd been squatting. A stream of smoke fizzled out in a charred spot of sand.

"What time is it?"

"Morning," he said.

"What the hell are you doing?"

"Ushering in the morning."

Then he took me by the arm and helped me to stand. Beneath his cape, tucked into the waist of his trousers, were three colourful roman candles.

"Where the hell did you get those?" I yelled.

"The gas station. Don't yell. I know exactly what I'm doing. I'm not you."

"We didn't buy those at that gas station. And it's daylight."

"Exactly."

I looked down at my feet, realizing how damp and cold they'd become. I started back to the tent.

"Wait, Julia," he said, grabbing my hand.

"What, did we not learn our lesson last night? I'm going to lose my toes."

"One more. Just watch. It's tradition."

"Tradition from when?"

He propped the firework to his mouth and made a trumpeting noise with his lips.

"That's not a trumpet," I said.

"Right. It's a firework. So let's light it."

I turned around again. After a moment, he ran after me. "Okay," he said. "Now, we take breakfast."

. . .

Over a new, small fire, Colt stirred a tin of miniature beige sausages into a pot of tomato soup. When he'd decided they were cooked, we ate the sausages, once again with stick chopsticks. Then took turns drinking the soup from the pot.

"We'll walk that way first, see what's past those hills."

He pointed his sticks in the direction of the train tracks.

"Colt, I can't," I started, but he held a sausage up to my mouth.

"Don't say it, Julia," he said. "There might be a water source there."

I took the sausage in my teeth and chewed. Held a hand to my forehead, squinted into the distance. Still a field. Still vacant.

"Even if there is, it's not like we can just drink it from the ground. It needs to be made drinkable."

He tapped the pot with his sticks.

"We'll run out of these canned goods, too, eventually," I said. "And one of us is going to get sick. And then get the other person sick, and then we're gonna be screwed because then neither of us will be able to go foraging for what little vegetation there is out here. We need to face the fact that eventually, we need to find life."

He held out the pot to me.

"Take it," he said.

I took it by the handle. He stood up and set to putting out the fire, scooping sand and throwing it on the embers. The sky was turning from grey to grey-blue. The sun was less than a third of the way up the sky. I wiped my running nose on my sleeve. Then looked up at Colt, who'd stopped throwing dirt and was looking down at me.

"Well?" he said.

"Well what?"

"You gonna finish that?"

I looked down at the last bit of soup. It didn't even fill the bottom of the pot. I sloshed it back and forth, disrupting the skin that was developing over the top. Then lifted it to my mouth and drank it. I looked back up at Colt and he nodded, once, as though in approval. Then took hold of the lowest branch and pulled himself up into the umbrella tree. Climbed through the leafy side, knocking leaves to the ground, and over to the barren side. Balancing himself between two branches, he made circles with his thumbs and fingers and held them to his eyes like binoculars. I set the pot on the ground. Then collapsed forward into the drop, cover, and hold position. The branches above moaned.

After a few moments, I raised my head. Colt was still up there, one arm around the trunk. I could feel the cold setting in deeper, so I pushed myself up to standing, shook my legs in my bell-bottom pants. Flapped my elbows a little, like wings. Then raised my arms above my head, waved them in circles, jumped jumping jacks, ran on the spot. Yapped like a dog. But couldn't shake it. Colt climbed down two branches and jumped.

"We'll see what's beyond the hills," he said again, facing the horizon. I looked back at the car. It looked like a car. But one that, if it could speak, would beg us to give it just one more day.

"Okay," I said.

"Okay."

He started toward the tent. I followed behind him. He crawled inside, then stopped me with a hand held up to my face.

"Password," he said.

I pushed his hand away. He began to button the flaps in front of me. I stuck my hands between to stop him.

"I forget," I said. "Something about a donkey?"

He sighed.

"No, that was the one I made up," I said.

"We'll go over this one more time. Owl-eyed eagle."

"Okay."

He stared at me.

"I say that now?" I said.

He dropped his head.

"Owl-eyed eagle. That doesn't sound right," I said.

"That's the password."

"Are you sure? I could have sworn it was something else."

"The woodpecker has landed."

"The woodpecker has landed," I repeated.

"You don't say that part."

"Right."

"The woodpecker has landed," he said again. Then he held open the flap. I crawled under his arm and sat on my knees. It was still warm inside. Amongst the stuff strewn over the floor, he found the dish towel, stained now with grease, sweat, and proceeded to tear it with his teeth.

"What are you doing with my towel?" I said.

"Our towel," he replied, spitting. He continued to rip the cloth into strips, tied one strip around his forehead, then reached over and did the same to me.

"Whatever we truly need we can find in the great outdoors," he said.

"Those weenies weren't from the great outdoors."

He sat back on his heels. Head pressed against the roof of the tent, his hair sticking straight up from the static.

"This is it, Julia." He jabbed his finger against the floor of the tent between us. "This is Egg Island. If it isn't the beginning of something, then it's the end."

I took a deep breath. Reached up and straightened the towel around his head. Then he crawled out from the tent, and I crawled out after him. Went over to the fire pit, scooped soot from the edge with his fingertips, turned to me and drew two lines across my cheeks. Then did the same to himself.

"While we're out there, stay close," he said. "Do not stray. Straying causes confusion. Which causes backtracking. Which causes wastes of time. We are stronger together. Four eyes. Four ears. Eight arms and legs."

"Eight of each or eight total?"

"Should any danger arise and we somehow ended up separated, regroup back at basecamp. Save yourself. Don't come looking for me."

He began to walk forward.

"Wait," I said.

He stopped, turned around.

"You mean just leave you behind?" I said.

"You can't be thinking that way when we're out there, Julia."

"Would you come for me?"

"That's a laughable question. Ha ha."

"If you would come for me, how come I can't come for you?"

He sighed again. Then stepped close, clasped me by the arms.

"I have a significantly higher body mass index than you," he said.

He turned and kept walking.

"What kind of danger do you even expect to come across?" I said.

Still marching, he raised a finger and pointed to the sky.

"Right," I said.

"Bring the pot," he called back.

. . .

Colt balanced along a rail. Hopped to the other in one bound. I followed, but in three. In front of us, a steep hill dotted with pine trees sloped upward. I held the bottom of his cape with one hand as if he were pulling me, and together, we climbed.

"You know what I really, really want right now?" I said, between breaths.

"A crossbow," said Colt.

"Pie. Can we find some in nature?"

"I could whittle a rock into a spear head. Construct the body using sticks and towel shreds."

We wove through the trees at the top over to the other side. On the other side, we discovered an identical green field with a single fat tree plunked dead centre.

"This reminds me of something, too," I said.

"Quiet."

He held a finger up to his lips. Cupped his ear.

"I can hear it," he whispered.

I listened, but couldn't hear anything. Except Colt's feet as he plodded down the other side of the hill. A moment later, his footsteps stopped.

"Julia," he called.

Some leaves fell to my head.

"What?" I shouted.

"Julia," he called out again, longer, and louder.

"What?" I shouted again. Also louder.

He didn't respond. I started down the hill. Soon the ground ahead began to flatten, and I could hear the gentle prattle of a river. Colt was on the other side of it when I emerged. It curled through the trees along the base of the hills. It seemed to go on forever in both directions. There was no lake in sight.

"Where did it come from?" I said.

"Throw me that pot."

I walked a short ways down the river to where a rock large enough to jump on stuck out from the water. I leapt, balanced. Then leapt to the other side. Went over to Colt and handed him the pot. He crouched down beside the river and rinsed it. The tin knocked against the pebbles. I walked out a bit into the field, watching the tree, half expecting to see two kids with towels wrapped around their heads and soot on their faces to be standing there, looking back.

"Julia," Colt whispered as loud as he could.

I turned around. Went over and knelt beside him.

"Yes?" I said.

"Look. Life."

He pointed to where a turtle the size of my hand rested on top of a rock. Set the pot down, then lay on his stomach to meet it at eye level.

"Hey there, little buddy," he said, still whispering. "What's your name?"

The turtle was quiet.

"Is this rock your house?"

The turtle was still quiet.

"Her name is Julia. Mine's Colt. We're going to be your parents from now on."

I dipped my fingertips into the water then lifted them to my nose.

"We're going to live here with you," he continued. "And love and support you, no matter what. If you want to be vegetarian, or get a tattoo. Even if you decide you don't want to be a turtle anymore. You wanna be an egret."

"Thanks, Dad," I said in as deep a voice I could muster. Colt frowned.

"You're going to scare him," he said.

He pushed himself back onto his knees, turned around to face the field, and sat with his legs stretched out in front of himself. Leaned back on his forearms. I lay down next to him on my stomach, pressed my cheek to the ground. The grass was cold. Wet. Colt's exposed shins were stippled with dirt. A small black bug crawled through the forest of his spindly black hairs. There were probably bugs crawling up through my pores, too. We were just part of the environment now.

"My grandpa gave me this great advice once. 'Be the cowboy, Colt,'" he said.

"Do you feel like a cowboy right now?"

"I'm being."

"If you're the cowboy, what does that make me?"

"A cowboy," he said.

"A cowgirl?"

"Cowboy."

I pushed myself up onto my forearms. Picked at the grass. Got dirt beneath my nails, where dirt was already stuck.

"What did your grandpa mean by that?"

"It's not something you find the meaning of. It's just something you put in your brain and keep there."

"Well, what were you doing when he said it?"

"I don't remember. Breaking something I cared about. Or something that he cared about. Can you imagine a cowboy being pissed off or sad? No."

"My dad told me once, 'Don't be a fool.'"

"That's important, too. Especially for you."

He leaned over and plucked a thick, rough weed from the ground. Held it up, popped the flower off the top, then stuck the stem in his mouth and began brushing it against his teeth.

"Can I tell you something else?" he said.

"I guess."

"Sometimes, I feel like I've been at this forever. And then I remember how long my grandma and grandpa were at it before she died."

"At what?"

"Jules, when we were at that last gas station, and I saw the guy who worked there, it made me think about how everything could have happened in a much different way, had you kept walking that first day and gone pee at the next gas station up the road from mine."

He offered me the weed.

"What kind of plant is that?"

"I'd thought about it before, too, but in a way where I didn't realize that was what I was thinking about. Until that last gas station. I realized that everything that's happened could have happened with you and that guy, and not you and me."

He sucked his teeth, spun the weed in his fingertips.

"Once you showed up with that water balloon inside of you, ready to burst from just one more step, time started moving funny. Like it was hyperventilating. That's why I believed in you from the start. It really feels like hours and minutes go really fast and can't breathe well, when we're together."

"Is that a good or bad thing?"

I could see him studying that tree in the distance. The space around it, beyond it.

"I'm sorry about your dad," he said. "He could've walked on, or ridden an off-roader, like that man said. If you want to think about it that way."

"I don't."

He nodded. "I wouldn't, either."

Then he pushed himself up onto his feet. Held out a hand to pull me up, too. I took it.

"Do you think you can carry that pot of water all the way back to basecamp without spilling it?"

"No."

"You're gonna try though, right?"

"What else would I do?"

He crouched down beside the river again.

"I still believe in you," he said, filling the pot with water. "And I believe in you, champ," he said to the turtle. "It's a long river, full of pebbles and bacteria and cold water. But you're the one with the shell. Don't forget that."

He looked up at me. Pushed his hair back from his face. I could see how greasy it was at the roots. I could see pimples around his eyebrows and his nose forcing their way up through the soot. And even though I didn't want to, I could also see the way he was looking at me, how it still hadn't changed from the fire the night before.

"Your turn," he said. "Anything you want to say to the little guy?"

"Yeah," I said. "You know, there may come a day when this is all covered in pavement and tall buildings. Stores. Flying cars. Flying sausage stands. It may seem like there's nothing but a whole lot of noise and bright lights, and it hurts to look at. So much so you might want to pull your head down into your esophagus and just look backward instead, forever, to a place where you can't see or hear anything at all. Except your own cloacal respiration. But as long as there's some water and mud around, you can probably survive another hundred years or so until it all turns back into earth. Because you're a turtle. You'll outlive us both. Don't forget that, either."

Colt nodded.

"Wise words from your mother," he said.

. . .

I lay on my back beneath the umbrella tree, watching the sky. Strange green and purple clouds twisted out from the horizon. West. Northwest. Colt sipped from the pot of water he'd boiled over the fire.

"Have you seen any birds lately?" I asked him.

"I haven't been looking."

"I don't think I've seen a single bird since we got here."

"They probably just migrated."

There was a warm breeze amidst the cold air. A leaf detached from a spur of a branch and drifted downward. I tracked it, trying to guess where it would land. Chose a dirt clod near my right foot. It proved me wrong.

"I'm thirsty again," I said.

Colt held the pot toward me. I sat up against the trunk of the tree.

"What about the other bottle? In the car?"

"That's for emergencies," he said.

"Is this not an emergency?"

"I don't feel emergent. Do you?"

"This pot'll run out soon."

"When the pot runs out we'll suck on these rocks."

He pulled two rocks from his pockets and showed them to me. Another leaf fell. This time, it landed in the pot of water. It was starting to get dark, as though the giant above was taking cover. I had no idea what time it was. The sun seemed to be in the same spot it had been when I first woke up in the tent.

"Tell me a story," I said.

"There was this man who lived alone in a house. It was a regular house. With a garage and new windows. On a regular street, in a regular part of a regular town. It was actually kind of a boring place. Even the kids there were kind of lame. They would do stuff like take your skateboard and throw it in the Dumpster behind the Crispy Wings, then cluck at you while you had to Dumpster dive through the chicken scraps and bones, and one time, even a neck and head with a beak. Actually, one time, even a whole bald baby chicken. With blood on it. The point is, the man who lived alone, he started noticing peculiar things happening in his otherwise super regular, boring existence. Like one day, he woke up and was going into the kitchen to make his regular coffee, and he noticed his favourite mug was missing. It's not like it was a nice mug. It was just white with some easy-listening radio station logo on it. But it was his favourite. So we have to respect that. Anyway, he supposed he'd just misplaced it, so he chose a different mug and carried on with his morning. But then, after he drank his coffee, he went to take a shit."

"Colt," I said.

"Wait, let me tell the story. He went to take a shit, and noticed that the toilet paper roll was all unravelled across the floor. And he didn't have a cat. That was the first day. Next day, he noticed a hole right through the middle of his loaf of bread. As if a bolt had been shot right through with a cross-bow. Then, a kitchen chair was missing. The bristles on his toothbrush were all burned off. *Maybe I have a sleepwalking disorder*, he thought to himself. *Why don't I schedule an appointment with my doctor, because that's what a regular person would do if they suspected a health concern*. So he wrote it on a little yellow sticky note, *Call doc in a.m.*, and stuck it on the call display. Because regular people are always trying to remember stuff they have to do in the a.m. and coming up with tricks in order to do so. So, a.m. comes, and the man wakes up and goes into the kitchen, and what does he find but none other than his favourite mug, right beside the coffee maker. But when he picks it up to give it a rinse, because he always pre-rinses his mugs out of dull, unspecial, characterless habit, what does he find? None other than the curly black telephone cord, all hacked up into bits and stuffed inside. And the yellow sticky note was lying in the sink, the ink all streaky from the dripping tap so he could barely even read the reminder. But that's not all. Then, he noticed the knife block. From which there was one knife missing. Which was none other than the meat cleaver."

He paused.

"Go on," I said.

"That's the big knife."

I nodded.

"Got it," I said.

"He opens the drawers. Checks the cupboards. Then he goes to the living room. Takes all the cushions off the couch. Goes to the bathroom. Looks in the back of the toilet. Looks under his bed. His panty drawer. No sign of any knife. So he thinks to himself, *All right, I'll just put on some boring clothes, get in my basic car, and drive to the store to buy a new phone, so I can call the doctor, and make my appointment.* So he gets dressed, gets his shoes on, opens the garage door. Unlocks his car. Opens the car door. Sits down inside the car."

"I get it," I said.

"Puts the key in the ignition. Starts the engine. Adjusts the mirror. And then."

He paused again.

"Was there someone in the back seat?"

"The garage door opened. He backed out. He drove down his regular, boring street. Went to the store and bought a new phone from some lame guy named Alex. Then he took his phone to his car. Opened the trunk. Put the phone inside the trunk. Got back in his car. Started the engine again. Backed out of the parking spot."

"And drove to his house?"

"Backed out of the parking spot. Drove to his house. Pulled into the garage. Parked the car. Turned off the engine. Got out of the car. Opened the trunk. Took out the phone. Closed the trunk. Locked the car, and went back into his house, where he plugged in the new phone. So. Then."

He stopped for a moment, thinking.

"He was going to call the doctor?" I said.

"He calls his doctor and says, 'Doctor? Yes. No, everything is fine. It's just that I believe I'm having some minor sleep issues.' And makes an appointment for the following day.

Then he dumps out the mug of hacked-up wire, brews some fresh coffee, and goes to his study and does boring stuff. Skip ahead to bedtime."

"What does he do during the day?"

Colt shook his head.

"I don't know, Jules. Crosswords? It doesn't matter. Skip ahead to bedtime. He goes to brush his teeth with a new tooth-brush. He also, at one point, went out to his car and drove to a store to get a new toothbrush. And new bread."

"Right."

"Just pretend I told you that part."

"It was a good part."

"So, he goes to sleep. And then, in the night, he has a dream. Usually his dreams are ordinary. Flies, dies. Whatever. But this dream, it's not an ordinary dream. It's a fucked-up dream."

Again, a warm breeze. It slipped between us, rustling Colt's hair.

"In this dream, he wakes up, and he's in his bed, in his room, in the middle of the night. Everything is exactly like how it is in real life, but he's really hungry. So he thinks, *Hey, why not make some toast?* And he gets out of bed and goes downstairs. And as he walks toward the kitchen, he hears a noise. Like someone, or something, is rummaging through his cereal cupboard. He takes a step and steps on something hard. He looks under his foot. Finds a macaroni noodle stuck to it. He takes another step, and steps on more macaroni noodles. The whole way to the kitchen, hard noodles sticking to his feet. When he gets to the kitchen, he turns on the light. And what does he see?"

I waited.

"What?" I said.

"What do you think he sees?" said Colt.

"Raccoon?"

"He turns on the light, and what does he see but none other than this little hunchback man, his limbs all bent the wrong way, his ears not even with each other on the sides of his head, sitting on the kitchen floor, dumping the pack of cheesy powder from a box of macaroni all over his face. Then he stops. Looks up at the man's eyes. And then, bam."

Colt clapped his hands in front of my face.

"Bam what?"

"The man wakes up. In his bed. And he's all sweaty and disgusting. He even shit in his fucking pants a little."

"What?"

"He gets out of bed, and he goes downstairs, and at the bottom of the stairs, what does he step on but an itty bitty teeny tiny teensy weensy raw macaroni noodle. He turns on the light. There's a trail of them leading into the kitchen. He grabs an umbrella from his umbrella stand near the door to use as a makeshift spear, and slowly, he walks toward the kitchen, following the noodles. Then he gets to the kitchen. Turns on the light."

He leaned in close to my face. I leaned back a bit.

"And there," he whispered, "in the kitchen, dumping Oaties into a jar of peanut butter and eating it with a spatula, was, none other than Uncle Fred."

His eyes and mouth all opened wide.

"Who's Uncle Fred?"

"My uncle Fred. He kind of goes on and off his meds sometimes and does stuff like break into my uncle Harris's house."

The northwest clouds were closing in on us now. And had developed shades of red and brown. They almost appeared to be spinning, like slot machines.

"Is this normal?" I said, pointing up at them.

Colt looked up. His skin was tinged orange in the light.

"I've definitely seen this before," he said.

"When?"

"In a dream."

The cold and warm winds braided through my hair. I felt a drop of rain on my cheek. The tree groaned.

"Did you feel that?" I said.

A drop hit his forehead and slid down into his eye.

"Feel what?" he said, blinking. Until his gaze fixed beyond me, toward the tracks in the distance. I turned around. A cloud like the trunk of an elephant slowly squirmed its way toward the hills.

"What do we do?" I said.

"Our turtle," said Colt.

I reached forward and clutched his cheeks.

"We need to go the other way now," I said.

His eyes shifted from the cloud to mine.

"Okay," he said.

Then rose, ran to the tent. I ran after him.

"Grab the clothes," I shouted. "The backpack."

"The password, Jules, the password," he shouted back.

"Really?"

"What's the point in having a system if you're never going to use it?"

I pushed through the door flap. The rain was coming in faster, battering the tent.

"The woodpecker has landed," he shouted.

"The dark side of nature has landed, Colt," I shouted as he grabbed the backpack. Then, tearing back the zipper, he found the map from the motel at the bottom of it.

"It's here," he said. "The map's here."

He reached his arm in. I pulled on the bottom of the backpack.

"No time, Colt."

"Why'd you say you didn't have it?"

I pulled harder until he let go. Then I bolted out from the tent to the car. Colt started to follow, then stopped. Turned back to the tent and started trying to dismantle it. I opened my door.

"Leave it," I shouted.

"I can't."

There was a boom and a crack. A large branch snapped, falling onto our firepit.

"Please," I shouted.

He stumbled sideways in the wind. Then went over to where the branch had just fallen. Grabbed the pot, then finally ran to the car. We shut our doors. His shoulders, legs, were soaked. Hair blown back off his face in a wet, tangled mess. He held the pot in his lap.

"Where are the keys?" I said.

Without looking, he reached over and punched the glove compartment. It fell open. Keys dropped to the floor. I picked them up and handed them to him. Another heavy wind shook the whole car. I looked out the back window. The tornado was weaving closer. Colt started the engine. We both took one last look at the umbrella tree as its remaining leaves shot from the branches, and the tent, as it lifted from the ground, flew up into the sky like a UFO.

XLI

· · · · · ·

"TELL ME A story," said Colt.

"There was this boy named Holt who lived in a car and was really skilled at harnessing the power of fire."

"You're not even trying."

"No, listen. He was really short and bald. And he had a dog."

"What kind of dog?"

"A hound dog."

"A golden retriever."

"Okay, he had a golden retriever."

Colt wiped his nose with his cape. We were pulled over on the side of the road, a few miles from the site of the storm. The sky had cleared, was once again a grey-blue heaven. A daytime moon. Even a few stars. The car heating as much as it could.

"One day Holt and his golden retriever go out on a mission to collect materials to build a sacrificial sculpture."

"For Hephaestus?" said Colt.

"Bless you," I said.

"To honour Hephaestus, god of fire."

"Yes. Exactly. So, sticks. Clippings from his uncle's shrubs."

"Flour from his uncle's cupboard."

"What?"

"It's highly flammable."

"Okay. Flour from his uncle's cupboard."

"And ping-pong balls. From his uncle's shed."

"Ping-pong balls are flammable?"

"They're made of concentrated celluloid. Same stuff as dolls from Titanic times. Can you picture it? Her glassy blue eyes looking up at you as her face melts into a gaping hole, crying, 'Save me, save me, Colt, or I'll come to life as a demon toy and cut your tonsils out with the turkey scissors.'"

"Okay. And ping-pong balls from his uncle's shed."

"The dog's name is Sam."

"That's what you'd name your dog?"

"That's what Holt would name his dog."

"So, Holt and Sam are out collecting stuff to create a controlled fire for the fire god when, for no reason it seems, Sam starts acting completely deranged. Like, rabies style. He breaks free from his leash and goes running off into the woods."

"Which woods?"

"The ones near his uncle's house?"

"Those ones aren't scary. The ones coming home from his uncle's house after you pass the highway are better."

"Holt goes chasing after him, into the woods that are past the highway, calling out, 'Sam, here Sammy Boy, come to Papa, Sammy Boy, I got some canned weenies for you.' And he walks deeper and deeper into the woods. It's getting darker, the deeper he goes. He can't see anything because the trees are so thick and dense. Then, after it feels like he's been walking forever, he hears this shrill little whine."

Colt bunched his cape in a fist beneath his chin. I whined like a scared dog.

"'Sam?' says Holt, 'What is it, boy? Come here, Sammy. Come to Pappy, my little boy.' More whining. 'Sam? Sammy?' He takes a few steps forward, when, through the trees, he sees a bright-green light, pulsating and moving toward him. Then, Sam the dog starts yelping."

I yelped.

"Stop it," said Colt.

"I haven't got to the good part yet," I said.

"You're not doing it right."

"Doing what right?"

"Nothing."

He straightened up in his seat and restarted the ignition. Then turned it off again. Drooped his forehead onto the steering wheel. I didn't know what to say. So I placed my hand on his back.

"How do I do it?"

"Don't hurt the dog," he said into the horn.

"What? No. In this story, Sam's fine. Trust me."

He turned his face to mine, cheek all smushed against the wheel.

"I know," I said. "I'm sad, too."

He rolled his eyes.

"No, really," I said. "I liked our tent. And our headbands. I liked how at night, the train sounded so close. As if it was gonna barrel right over and disembowel us like two tubes of toothpaste."

He smiled, a squished half smile. I picked up the pot from the floor beneath my feet.

"I like cooking with this pot, too," I said. "Well, watching you cook with this pot. We'll find a new place. With a new hill to climb. Maybe we'll even find another turtle. It's what we do."

He sat up straight and took a deep breath. Then opened his door. Got out. Marched straight down the road ahead, not stopping until he was at least five car lengths away. Then turned around. Pushed back his cape and pulled the remaining roman candle from the waist of his trousers. Lit the wick with the lighter he'd plucked from thin air, raised his arm, and held the firework straight up to the sky.

XLII

I WOKE UP shivering in the back seat. Fog coated the insides
of the windows. In the front, Colt was still very much asleep,
mouth hanging open, breathing slowly. I sat up, cranked the
window down. It felt warmer outside than in the car. I rested
my chin on the bottom of the frame. Stuck out my tongue and
tasted the air. Tasted better, too. All the space around us seemed
tranquilized now. As though it'd just come out of surgery.

Colt opened his eyes.

"I'm awake," he said.

"Go back to sleep."

He shifted his seat upright. Rubbed his face with both
hands.

"Go back to sleep," I said again.

"It's a new day," he said. "Anything could happen."

"What do you think is going to happen?"

His stomach rumbled.

"The point isn't to think," he said. "It's to drive. Hand me
those marshmallows."

. . .

The next life we encountered was selling unshucked corn and a variety of peculiarly small trees from the back of an open van. We walked up the side of the road, having left the car parked farther down where we'd decided to stop. The road was gravel, muddy, and the bell bottoms of my pants were like two mopheads swishing up the muck. Colt walked with his hands tucked in the pockets of his trousers, high up near his belly button.

Next to the van, beneath a wide-brimmed straw hat, a man sat with his legs outstretched and ankles crossed, arms folded up at his chest, in a folding lawn chair. The blue-and-white webbing split and frayed all along the edges.

"I bet that'd burn well," said Colt.

Once he realized we were approaching, the man stood and bowed. We bowed in return.

"Hi, friend," Colt said to the man. "We were just passing through when we noticed your corn here. How much for a couple of cobs?"

"Five for six," the man said, holding up five, then four, then six fingers.

Colt turned to me.

"Well, lady, what do you say?"

Ignoring him, I stepped closer to examine the trees arranged along the edge of the van's floor and atop overturned boxes set near the tires. Imagined them filling a circle in the middle of a cornfield. The man picked up a very small one with hot-pink blossoms popping from the dark-green bush.

"For you," he said. "Bonsai."

I held the ceramic pot in the palm of my hand.

"What does it do?" I said.

He shrugged.

"For you," he said again. "Pretty."

I turned to Colt, who was bent over a bushel examining corn.

"Look," I said to him.

He twisted sideways to see me.

"How tall will it get?" he said.

I turned to the man.

"How much will it grow?"

The man knocked a pack of cigarettes out from the breast pocket of his jacket. Shook his head no, and placed a cigarette up behind his ear. Colt watched him, then stood up straight.

"Excuse me, sir," he said. "Could I borrow one of those?"

The man looked at Colt, then at the pack.

"Yes. One of those," Colt said.

He shrugged and shook out another cigarette. Handed it to Colt, who also placed it up behind his ear.

"How much for this tree?" I said to the man.

"Fifty. Five-oh," he said.

"Hm," I said, looking up at Colt.

"Indeed," said Colt. Then, to the man, he asked, "Could you tell us, sir, if there's some place around these parts where a couple of folks could get their fill?"

The man pointed a spindly finger out to the field across the road.

"Sign with black marker. Church with no door."

Colt looked out at the field for a moment, then back to the man.

"Right or a left?"

"Tree with many shoes," said the man.

"Gotcha," said Colt. Then took the tree from my palm and set it, lopsided, on top of some corn. He bowed again. "Much obliged. Thanks, friend."

I bowed again, too.

. . .

On our way back to the car, Colt held the cigarette between two fingers, drawing it up to the centre of his lips and pretending to inhale.

"Smoking is delicious," he said. "I'm so relaxed."

"Why don't you light it?" I said.

"This way I can reap the benefits without all the asthma."

I stepped in front of him, stopping him. Took the cigarette from his fingers and placed it in my mouth. Then shoved my hand into his pocket and pulled out his lighter. Lit it, puffed, and watched the white smoke stream from my lips in a thin, gentle whirlwind. Then held it out to him. He took a step backward.

"I don't want to end up with a hole in my throat," he said.

"One puff," I said. "Don't be a chicken's, I don't know. Breast."

"That's stupid."

I shrugged, then dropped the cigarette on the ground. But as I went to step on it he pushed me away. Bent over and picked it up with his thumb and forefinger. Held it for a moment and watched the ash build up on the tip. Then shook it off, and placed the cigarette between his lips. Made a sucking noise as he inhaled.

One second later he was buckled over, puking. I held his hair while he heaved and spit a puddle of steamy yellow and white marshmallow bile at his feet. Once it was all out, he sat down beside his puddle, still holding the burning cigarette.

"I just need to sit down because I am so relaxed," he said.

I took the cigarette from him and threw it in the puddle. He wiped his mouth with his cape.

"Where'd you learn to smoke so good?" he said.

"Smoking class."

He cleared his throat.

"Don't tell anyone I yakked," he said.

· · · ·

We passed a can of beans back and forth, tipping it into our mouths.

"Does that map of yours show the tree with many shoes?" said Colt.

I hung my feet out the open car door.

"I'm sure we'll find it if we just keep driving," I said.

"I'm thirsty," he said.

I picked up the bottle of emergency water from the floor. There was one drop left. Wiped the dirt from off the top and handed it to him.

"There's a drop in there," I said.

He shook it over his mouth. Then squeezed the bottle in his fist, twisting it, trying to form it into a ball. Then chucked it out the window.

"Don't litter," I said.

"I'll get it after."

"Drink the bean water," I said.

He dumped some more beans in his mouth. I stuck out my hand for the can.

"Wait," he said. "Look at me."

I looked at him over my shoulder.

"All the way," he said. "Turn and face me with both eyes."

I shifted in my seat.

"Now close them," he said.

"Absolutely not."

He laughed.

"What are you going to do?" I said.

"Tear off all your clothes and dump this can of beans on you and rub them all over your naked body. Julio Burrito, is what I'll call you."

I climbed out from my seat, backed away from the car.

"Come back, Julio," he said, gesturing me closer with a curling pointer finger.

"One of these days I'm going to have you arrested," I said.

"I've always wanted to escape from a prison. Come here."

I walked back to the car. Leaned inside.

"Close your eyes," he said.

I closed my eyes.

"Open your mouth."

"Ew."

"Tick tock," he said.

After a few seconds, I opened my mouth. I felt Colt's hand beneath my chin as he tilted it upward, then rested the can on my bottom lip. A lump of beans dropped out onto my tongue.

"Keep your eyes closed," he said, letting go. "Now, think about pie."

I frowned, mushing the beans against the top of my mouth.

"Sweet, soft blueberry pie with creamy whipped cream on top."

I mushed more. Then opened my eyes. He was still barely an inch from my face.

"Exquisite, or what?" he said.

"Tastes like cold beans," I said.

He sat back in his seat. I sat back in mine and pulled the door shut. He started the car. Then turned it off again.

"Where's the map?" he said.

"Cowboys don't need maps. We use our intuition."

"Cowboys use their senses, not their intuition."

"So let's sniff out the gas station."

"Why are you hiding it?"

"Hiding what?"

"The map."

He tapped the can against the steering wheel. I gestured for more.

"No more pie for you until you tell me what's going on," he said.

I sighed, looked down at the dash, the stereo. Thought for a moment. About a church with black marker. Or was it a black door. A door with a sign. A woodpecker. A donkey. I climbed between the seats, into the back, dug through my bag for the pen and pad of dental paper.

"You getting more marshmallows?" he said.

On the bottom right corner of the first page, I drew an X. Above it, in the centre of the page, I drew another X. Then a dotted line between them. Then I tore the page from the pad and started again. This time, I drew a star, and above it, a dollar sign. To the left of that, a bat, and above that, a window. I tore off this page, as well, and handed them both to Colt. He held one in each hand, watching as I continued. An arrow pointing up to a gun, which was pointed at a bottle of nail polish. Next page, a wagon wheel below a cracked egg, adjacent to a cup of tea. Then a peace sign. Then a phone. A sad face. A snowflake. Then I left one page blank, and on the next, I drew a plate with scribbles all over it.

"What's this one?" he said.

"Breakfast," I said.

"What are these scribbles supposed to be?"

"Eggs. Ketchup."

"Give me that pen," he said.

I handed him the pen. He flipped the page over and drew a new plate, but with a spiral in the middle, and fluffy little cloudlike circles all over. He tossed the pen back to me. On the new, blank page, I drew another X. Then a dotted line travelling down toward a triangle. Then another dotted line, toward another X. I handed the last sheets of paper to Colt.

Then, I climbed out of the car. Colt followed. One at a time, I directed him to hand me the drawings, which I arranged on the window, fastened down with the windshield wipers. I pointed at the first X.

"I woke up in the middle of the night. Was shook awake by I don't know what. A sound, like someone had just said my name inside my ear. Inside my brain. It wasn't real. I knew that after a couple seconds, when I sat up to drink some water. But there wasn't any in the cup beside my bed, so I got out of bed. To go get more. When I went to the hall, I saw a light from the living room. Not a lamp, more like a flashlight. Because it was moving. I thought there was a burglar in the house. And I wanted to scream, but I was too scared. I was kind of frozen, really. Holding my empty cup. Then I think I started thinking of what objects I had in my room that I could use as a weapon. That's when I saw him."

"Uncle Fred."

"My dad. Winter boots and a golf shirt. Carrying a stuffed hockey bag. He was looking for his map."

"Your dad plays hockey?"

"No. I mean, he hadn't in a really long time. Colt, he was going. He'd packed his snowsuit. His turn was up."

He looked away from the windshield for a moment, over his shoulder.

"I'd hidden his map because he'd told me, not too long before. He said something was changing. There was a coldness he couldn't shake inside himself. Like an object. A cold, round object in his stomach. Like a dead rock. I knew what that meant. But he didn't. Not what it really meant. And really, I knew no stupid piece of folded-up paper would stop what was about to happen. Like trying to hide from a tornado beneath an umbrella."

Colt's cape quivered. I pointed at the last X on the final page I'd drawn.

"That cornfield we broke down beside is adjacent to us now. Three and a half kilometres east. We're going to keep going this way until we get to the road that'll connect us back to that road we were on. Past the town with the library. We don't want to stop there again. But we will find a place to stop. Get gas and some water. And something real to eat, if there's anything to steal. Then we're gonna have to drive a little farther."

I dragged my finger along the glass. It made a squeaking noise.

"The roads are gonna get windy and rocky, and the forests are gonna get more thick. There will be more towns, too, closer together. Soon, we'll get to another gas station."

I placed my finger back on the first sheet, next to the second *X*.

"We're gonna stop again. You're gonna go back to work at that gas station."

Colt looked up from the papers.

"And save up all your money," I said. "Lots of it. Hundreds. And I'll get a job, too. In my town. I can pour slushies or do kiddie birthday parties at the bowling alley. I'll work every day and night that I can. I'll even work both at the same time. And then, we'll take our money and buy a better car. And a better tent. And like, equipment. Like, coolers, and those heavy duty flashlights. And those clip things you attach to your backpack so you can carry more stuff. And better backpacks, obviously. An air mattress. And I'm going to learn to drive. For real. I'm going to take driving lessons and get a real licence."

"Are you even old enough to get a licence?" said Colt.

Then, a gust of wind. The papers whipped against the window.

"Maybe we'll go WWOOFing," I said.

"What's WWOOFing?"

Another gust, but this one stronger. Too strong, and the wipers didn't hold. One bent back, nearly popping off. Colt ran onto the road, chasing after the little white squares of stationery. I went after him. One of the papers blew up from the road and stuck to my stomach. I grasped it in my palm and held it there. Then I looked over at Colt, who'd managed to rescue the rest. He stood up and walked toward me, shoving the now crinkled and dirtied papers into his pocket. I held out the sheet in my hand. My scribbles, his skillfully refined scrambled eggs.

"Here," I said.

He took the paper. Crammed it into his pocket with the others. Then we sort of just stood there in silence, together, but across from one another in some vast, open space, a little ways down from a corn and bonsai tree stand.

"That was close," he said.

"Yeah."

"We almost lost another map."

"Yeah. I know."

"So, it's a plan," said Colt.

"It's a plan," I said.

Then he wrapped his arms around me. I pressed my nose against his mouldy Hawaiian shirt. We were both so foul smelling, so filmy. So sweaty, even though it was cold. His cape blew up around us, hugging us closer.

"Or, we can stay right here," he said. "Live off corn and cigarettes."

"Like cowboys," I said.

"Not like. Be."

Colt always knew the right thing to do.

XLIII

· · · · · · · ·

IN A SMALL parking lot, we sat on the hood of the car, sipping from a bottle of water, pulling bits from the cross of a hard hot cross bun. Inside, the route home was spread open across Colt's seat. We had two coins left now, half a dollar in total, which I held in my hand. Before leaving, I gave one to Colt, and we walked over to a puddle in some fractured pavement. Made our wishes and chucked them both.

The roads did get more windy and rocky. And the forests did get more thick. But we could see through a lot of that thick now, as the leaves died. They blew all over the road. It was still cold, but not like before. It was a warm cold. Even though the clouds were dark a lot of the time, they felt more like blankets than curtains over the window to the unknown. In intervals, it would rain hard. The first time it happened, Colt reached his arm out the window to snap the busted wiper back into place. It worked for five minutes. The second time, it snapped right off. After that, it became a sword for him to stab my ribs and ear with. Then a wand, with which to cast dummy spells on me. But whenever we stopped for rest, it became a drumstick. That was the worst.

I stayed awake as much as I could with Colt, who kept on driving through the night, which seemed to arrive earlier than it ever did before. When the clouds broke up, we would see lights in the sky. Planes and satellites. We would see the flickering tops of radio towers in nearby places. The next thing to go was the left tail light. Then something below Colt's seat was making a rumbling sound. One quick piss break led to an hour of trying to restart the engine. The wheels were low on air.

As it happened, though, we made it to the next station. Slowed to a stop a little ways up the road. I could see the two pumps. The brown wood exterior. The deteriorating door to the restroom. The windows above the store that must have looked outward from Colt's grandpa's home. From Colt's home. The curb where I'd sat. The *open* sign hung crooked on the doorknob. Colt was quiet for a long time. Until he whistled. A long, sinking whistle.

"I can't go in there," he said.

"Why does it look so different?"

"I don't know."

He inhaled. Then whistled again.

"Why are you doing that?" I said.

"I whistle when I'm nervous."

"I've never heard you whistle before."

"You've never seen me nervous before."

We sat there a while longer. He drummed with his fingers on the steering wheel. Then he found the wiper I'd tried to shove deep between the seats and out of sight, and started drumming with that.

"Do you think he can see us parked here?" I said.

"He wouldn't be looking."

He drummed harder, his other hand holding his lit lighter as he thrashed. Then, he started thrashing his head. I grabbed the end of the wiper blade.

"This isn't safe," I said.

He let go of the blade, looked down at his lighter. Then looked out the window, flicking the lighter near the glass.

"If I go see my grandpa now it'll make me too sad, and I won't be able to leave again."

I tapped the blade against the glove compartment. The door dropped open. A driver's manual slid out and onto the floor, dragging some tissues and cough drop wrappers with it. I picked it all up, shoved it back in, and pushed the door up. It dropped open again.

"Just leave it," said Colt. "It wants to be open. Let it be open."

I let it be open.

"What if," he started. Then stopped.

"What?"

"Nothing. It was a moronic idea."

A car pulled into the gas station.

"What if you were the new window washer? Or ice cream scooper? Or parking lot garbage picker?"

"Here?" I said.

"I hate all those jobs. You'd be good at them. Great, even."

The door to the gas station opened, and the old man I barely remembered, skinny, lanky, with a slight hunch, emerged. He was wearing the same wool trousers as Colt. I was certain that at one point, he'd stood very tall. That he'd had dark eyes and long, ungroomed hair. Probably not an eyebrow ring, though. But maybe some kind of sailor tattoo. He walked over to one of the pumps and picked up the nozzle. Colt turned his face away, squeezed his eyes shut.

"Tell me when it's over," he said.

The old man placed one hand on the car while he pumped, as if he needed it for balance. After a minute, gave the nozzle a shake, then hung it back up. Went to the driver's window, collected his money, and nodded his head a bunch in thanks. Then waved as the car drove away. He stood there for a moment afterward, hands at his sides, one clutching the bills. Colt was right. He wouldn't look in our direction. He went back inside.

"You can look now," I said.

Colt opened his eyes. They were kind of red, like he'd been swimming. He started the car and pulled out from the curb.

"We're outta here," he said.

He started driving, fast. He drove for about one-and-a-half minutes, until the gas station was clear out of sight. Then pulled over again.

"So?" he said.

This time, I wanted to ask him what I looked like in that moment, looking back at him. If he could see that what I wanted more than anything was to go back and redo the parts we'd missed doing together. To climb back in through that washroom window and go forward, while our stomachs were still happy, stuffed with blueberry pie, into our whole, brief future of no missing parts.

"If I'm going to leave again, I have to do it right," I said. "Like, get some more underpants. And some other clothes I like. I have to tell them to be good, too. The twins. For some reason, I'm the only one they listen to."

XLIV

THE TREES BECAME organized. Evenly spaced amongst fire
hydrants and telephone poles. The roads were all paved now,
and well marked. Decorative planters with shrubs sticking out
of them prettied up the gaps between trash bins and phone
booths. These were things I had never really noticed before.

At the top of town there was a mall. Passing by it with
Colt felt wrong. The car felt wrong amongst the other cars
at the traffic lights, who were turning into the field of other
cars parked in front of the mall. The restaurants, in buildings shaped like boxes, with their oversized plastic signage
and drive-thru lineups, felt wrong. Even though I was starved.
Even though all I'd eaten in days was canned food from a shelf
where they'd been sitting for who knows how long. Decades,
probably. People on the sidewalks carried shopping bags. They
waited at bus shelters for a bus I knew would arrive at eleven
minutes past the hour, to dump a new load of people at the
mall, fill up, and circle the town again.

"Where's the bowling alley?" said Colt.

"In the mall," I said.

He drove in stops and starts. Like he wasn't certain of how to do it. Or like there were stop signs everywhere, which there were. In the middle of town there was a school. A crossing guard in an orange vest stopped us at a crosswalk. Children in colourful coats and hats and light-up shoes crossed in front of us, dragging their school bags. A boy wearing winter boots was trying to bounce a too-big basketball as he walked, and it rolled away from him, toward the car. He ran toward us and disappeared beneath the hood. The crossing guard blew his whistle and shouted. We both leaned forward to look out the window. The boy's head popped up, but he didn't bother to look at us. Just ran back to the crosswalk, wobbly, trying to carry his ball.

Lining the street near the school were bags of raked-up leaves plopped at the ends of long driveways. The houses near the school were the medium houses. Because they were fine. Colt drove extra slow, hunched up on the steering wheel, frowning.

"Look at these thugs," he said.

Ahead, a group of three teenagers was walking on the road. Two girls wearing tight sweaters and extremely loose jeans, one boy with a very large sweater and also extremely loose jeans. I sank low in my seat.

"It's immature to walk on the road like that," said Colt.

He honked the horn. They kept on, as if they hadn't heard. He honked again.

"Stop," I said.

"It's immature to ignore people when they're honking at you."

After the second honk, one of the girls did stop walking and turned around. She squinted at us through the windshield. Then her mouth dropped open. And her gum fell out. Her friends kept walking. Eventually, we were caught up with her, driving slow as she walked alongside us, staring at me. Finally, she just knocked on my window. Colt stopped the car. I rolled the window down.

"Um, Julia?" she said.

"Hi, Rayleen," I said.

"Is that you?"

"It's me."

She moved her mouth, chewing the gum that was no longer inside.

"You're like, so skinny," she said.

"Yeah. I'm pretty hungry, so."

"Julia, your mother called? And I covered for you, like you said to, but you also said it would just be for the weekend? You said you'd be back Monday? But clearly, you were not back Monday. In fact, several Mondays have happened since that particular Monday happened. Like, at least two. So, obviously, she called again, and at first I told her you were living with me for a while, like in my room, on the floor? Because you were sad? Because of your dad? But, to be honest, I don't think she believed me. Because then, school started, and honestly, I thought you'd died, and so she could probably hear it in my voice, that I thought that. So, then I told her I didn't know anymore. And then, I think, maybe, she started looking for you. Is this your boyfriend?"

Colt waved. She scrunched her face as if she'd just smelled beans.

"No," I said.

"Okay. She also told me to tell you that she's sad, too. If I heard from you."

"Okay."

"I'm glad you're not dead, Julia. And I'm glad you didn't get a boyfriend and not tell me. I think you look great, by the way. Sorry about what I said, about how you looked. Where did you even go?"

"Egg Island," said Colt.

"Eggs?" said Rayleen. "J, when can we hang out?"

"Not sure yet," I said.

Her friends were many bags of leaves ahead at that point. She looked up at them, chewing on her chipped green thumbnail now, instead.

"W and B would stop if they knew it was you. One hundred percent. Don't take it personal."

"I don't," I said.

She peered in at Colt again.

"Who are you?" she said.

"Roads are for wheels," he said.

She looked at me.

"What does he mean by the things he says?"

"Don't worry about it, Rayleen," I said.

She pulled a pack of gum from the back pocket of her jeans and popped a new piece into her mouth. Then offered the pack to me. I held up my palm. She popped a piece into it.

"Mrs. Butt put Terri Wachowski beside me in science. And like, she's okay to sit with, but still. Maybe Mrs. Butt will consider switching you and her, now that you're back. And also, we've been using your locker as a second locker. W and B and me. For our lunches and track stuff. Only because we thought you were dead. Honestly. I hope that's okay. You kind of deserve it, anyway."

She blew a bubble and popped it with her finger. Then stood there picking the gum from her nail.

"I do," I said.

Finally, her friends realized she was missing and stopped walking. She waved at them.

"Rayleen," I said. "Don't tell them it was me. Please."

She scoffed.

"I'm not covering up for you ever again, Julia Bermuda Tillerman. I've lied enough for a whole lifetime at this point. I'm definitely going to hell because of you."

I looked over at Colt. He turned the key in the ignition. Twice. The car restarted on the third try.

"Your friends better move out of the way," said Colt. "I'm about to show them what a road is really meant for."

He revved the engine. It sputtered. Rayleen made another bean face. I opened my mouth to say something to her, but couldn't think of the right thing to say. Because it felt wrong, too, being on the street with the medium houses. Being near her and the others. So I popped the gum in my mouth. Then reached my hand out the window. She took it in hers. She was wearing at least eight different mood rings.

"I love your rings," I said.

But what I should have said was thank you.

. . .

At the bottom of town were the small houses. On the outside, they seemed less than fine. Some were less than fine on the inside, too. But some were made up to be fine, or even nice. Depended on who lived inside. Mrs. Pierce's house, for instance, was fine inside, because she and her dead husband had never had kids. Before he died, it could even have been considered nice. Last time I saw it, though, it had needed a

cleaning. Which was why I'd been there. To help her bag stuff
up into trash bags, then move those trash bags to the donation
bins. And Gina's house was nice, because she'd renovated. And
Mr. Conway's because he said the neighbourhood would soon
see an increase in property value. I didn't know when that was
supposed to happen. On the small street, there were leaf bags
at the end of some shorter driveways. But there were also leaves
yet to be raked. And unbagged trash. And a busted miniature
hockey net that had blown out onto the middle of the road.
Colt plowed it out of the way with the front of the car.

At the end of the small street was an abandoned lot that
was sometimes referred to as the forest, and that actually
used to be a basketball court. Grass and weeds had long since
broken through the asphalt, left to grow wild. In the summer,
the forest was yellow with dandelions. Right now, it was dead
brown and grey. Tucked deep in the far corner of the forest and
almost out of sight was a blue tent and a grocery cart stuffed
with broken-down boxes and clothes of the sort Mrs. Pierce
had chucked for donation. Old suits and Christmas sweaters,
dress shoes, ties. It was where Mordecai lived. We almost never
saw him. He slept during the day. The only places in town we
didn't pass were the stations, fire station and police station,
the hospital, some plazas with vets, clinics, ATMs, everything
for cheap stores, the big rug store, the big furniture store, the
tall office building with the clock on top, and of course, the
YMCA. And the other school. The high school. That was it.

The house I came from, on the small street, did not have a
bag of leaves at the end of the driveway. There were, however,
two small piles and two small plastic rakes, blue and pink,
the spokes of which were contorted, maybe even chewed up.
There was also a shallow hole in the middle of the yard, and a

half-squashed rotting pumpkin dumped inside the hole. Colt drove the two right wheels onto the yard, in the tracks where other wheels had been parking for years. I unbuckled my seatbelt. Reached behind the seat for my backpack.

"This won't take long," I told him.

I looked up at the house. Halloween stickers were stuck crooked and upside down along the bottom of the window, a string of orange and black garland falling off the front door. A cardboard skeleton taped to the brick was missing an arm. I glanced over at Colt, then at myself in the side view mirror, hoping to see that I, too, looked wrong here. All I could see was that I needed a bath. So I opened the door and climbed out of the car.

"If I'm not back in ten, honk," I said, then walked away, across the lawn, over the leaf piles and the hole. It felt like I was wearing massive, ridiculous clown shoes. Or dreaming. But really, it was that time had slowed, instantly, now that I was out, and Colt was still inside of the car.

As I turned the knob, I felt it twist on the other side. I let go and the door swung open. Michael and Zen were pushing against each other and fake crying. Each had one hand on the knob, the other holding a chocolate popsicle that dripped down their wrists, hands, and onto the floor. There was chocolate all over their faces, like rings of poo around their mouths.

"Stop fighting," I whispered.

They frowned. Quieted their sobbing, but continued pushing. I stepped inside and separated them.

"I get you popsicle, Juya," Zen said.

"No, thank you," I said.

Then Michael hit his brother over the head. Zen screamed.

"I get hers popsicle!" Michael screamed over him.

He ran to the kitchen. Zen ran after him. I heard the freezer door hit the wall as they yanked it open. From the top of the stairs, I heard Mom shout, "You little shits, I said stay out of the fridge!"

"Is for Juya," Michael yelled.

Then a thud, the sound of a small cranium hitting the tiled floor. Mom came running down the stairs, stopping two short of the bottom once she saw me. She placed a hand over her heart. It made me too sad to see that. So I looked away from her, at the wall above the couch, where there was a hole, like someone had chucked a melon at it in an attempt to break through.

"You look at me," she said.

I turned my gaze to her bare feet. Her yellow calluses. Poppy-red toenails.

"Up here," she said.

Her black-and-pink polka-dotted tights. Gigantic Minnie Mouse T-shirt. She was pointing two fingers at her eyes. She wasn't crying. Or clenching. It was the look she had when I was caught. Like I'd made her feel stupid but she had to act the opposite. It looked sort of like she was reading a bill. Michael and Zen reappeared from the kitchen, each with one hand gripping either end of a wrapped popsicle.

"Don't lie to me," she said. "I will bludgeon you with a frying pan. Don't think I won't do it."

"I was sleeping on her floor."

She took the last two steps. I held my hands up.

"Don't hit me," I said.

"Take your shoes off."

Behind her, Michael gave one hard shove to Zen, knocking him to the ground. Zen screamed so loud he started choking on his own spit. His face was turning purple. Michael didn't look back at him once as he walked over to me, squeezing the popsicle in his closed fist.

"Here," he said.

He pressed it against my stomach, then let go. It fell to my feet. I bent down and picked it up. The wrapper was wet and cold. It left a wet, cold rectangle on the front of my sweater. I could feel that the popsicle inside had melted to broken chunks of mush. I set it in the basket that still hadn't moved, on top of a lonesome black glove, next to the map of Florida. Mom roared. Picked it back up.

"Jesus, Julia, don't you know how to use a coaster?"

Then whipped the popsicle at the coffee table, where it slid onto the floor, knocking a flimsy cardboard coaster down with it. She went over and picked up Zen, carried him back to me. He reached out. Wrapped his legs around my hips, arms around my neck. I'd lost the strength to carry him. Or he'd grown. He hiccuped between sobs. Rubbed his snot into my hair. Then Mom kneeled down on her knees and wrapped her arms around us both. Michael crawled over on all fours and started pawing at my legs, begging for a turn to be held. He hit me in the back of the knee and I lost my balance. Collapsed, dropping Zen, and toppling Mom. Michael climbed onto my back then, knocking my forehead against the metal vent on the floor. I fought my way out from under the pile, surfacing on the other side, facing the door I'd left from and returned through and was supposed to be walking out of once again. Mom pushed herself up. The boys continued to wrestle. She stepped over them and pulled me close. She smelled like chlorine and dish soap. And blush powder. And hair spray. The car horn honked.

"Who's honking?" she said. Then she let go of me and went to the window. Pulled back the curtain. I could see Colt in the car, watching the house like a spy.

"What a rude asshole," she said.

"He's not trying to be rude."

"Do you know him?"

I shook my head no.

"What is he, some kind of boyfriend?" Her voice rose. "Did that boy kidnap you?"

"No," I said. "He's good."

"I'm calling the police."

She spun in a circle. And then in another circle.

"Where's the cordless?" she yelled. "Find the phone, Julia."

"Stop," I yelled back. "Stop spinning and I'll explain."

She stopped, holding both hands out to her sides like she was carrying two imaginary serving trays. Or like she was about to look up, hoping the answers would come raining down from above.

"Who is that boy, Julia?" she cried.

"Colt."

"And?"

I sighed. Very deep. Then pretty much whispered.

"I thought I knew where to go. To find him."

She dropped her hands. Looked over my shoulder, at the hole in the wall. Level with my head. As though if I were to keep backing up, I'd sink right through, too. She switched her face to one of resolve, as if resolving in her head to make sure to finally patch it.

"He helped you?" she asked.

"Yes."

"He's nice?"

"Yes."

She turned and looked back out the window. At the nice boy parked out front. Then found the phone on the floor, next to my popsicle.

"Go thank him, then," she said, dialling. "I'm telling them you're home."

· · ·

I walked back outside, across the lawn, over the hole, and met Colt at the car, where he was rolling down the passenger side window.

"Where's your stuff?"

Behind me, at the window, they were watching. I didn't need to see to know.

"Inside."

"Go get it. Time is money, Jules. You taught me that."

"No, I didn't."

He leaned forward to look past me. Behind him, my flannel shirt was flattened into the crevice of his seat.

"That's your family," he said.

"No. Those are just some people I met in that house that I've never been inside of before."

He sighed the way I had inside the house. Collapsed sideways onto the passenger seat. I reached through the window and brushed the hair from his face. He squeezed his eyes shut, held them like that, then reopened them. Then did it again. Blinking repeatedly, as if he were trying to fall asleep and wake back up someplace else. In a bunk bed, or a tent. A black road beneath the stars. And to be honest, I was doing the same thing. As if he were on to something.

"It was Matt," he said.

I opened my eyes.

"Matt?"

"The information booth guy. He was the one who told me time is money."

"Colt, it's a saying. A lot of people say that. You've probably heard it like a trillion, billion times in your lifetime so far."

"A billion is less than a trillion," he said.

"Whatever."

He sat up. Shook his head. Pushed the hair back from his face. Then opened his door and climbed out. Walked around to where I was and stood right in front of me, just a single inch away.

"We're gonna save up our money," I said, looking up at his chin. "And buy a new car. And a new tent. Everything we need. I'm going to get a real licence. It's going to work."

"I know," he said. And it sounded like his voice was falling from the sky. Another sphere, even, he was just so tall. Seemed like it took forever for it to finally land. When it did, he pulled me into his chest by the back of my head. Then let go. Went back around the car, back into the driver's seat. And I turned away and walked toward the house. Because he couldn't look at me anymore. I couldn't look at him, either. We didn't need to. We'd figured it out, how to see each other perfect from that point, regardless.

Acknowledgements

. . . .

INFINITE GRATITUDE TO the Toronto Arts Council, the team at Dundurn Press, Sam Hiyate, Russell Smith, and my dearest friends and family.

To Mark Manner (and little Cheesy) — thanks for sticking with me every step of the way.

About the Author

SARA FLEMINGTON'S FICTION has appeared in publications such as *sub-Terrain*, the *Humber Literary Review*, the *Feathertale Review*, and others. She graduated from York University's Creative Writing program and completed her MFA at the University of Guelph. *Egg Island* is her first novel. Sara lives in Toronto.